CAR-CRAZY
GIRL

CAR-CRAZY
GIRL
BY HILA COLMAN

WILLIAM MORROW & COMPANY   NEW YORK 1967

Published simultaneously in Canada by George J. McLeod Limited, Toronto

Printed in the United States of America.

Library of Congress Catalog Card Number 67-19244

CAR-CRAZY
GIRL

1

She was glad the color of the car was red. Dina's car. That's what it would be called. The neat, new license plate said so: *D I N A*. She hated people who gave inanimate objects names. The ones who put silly signs like Easy Acres or Fowler's Folly on houses. Tasteless affectation. Unsophisticated.

"It's smashing," Jed said. He was in the driver's seat, pushing buttons, making the windshield wipers go back and forth, turning lights on and off. Then he blew the horn, loud and clear.

"What a lovely horn!" Dina jumped with ecstasy, wishing they would all go away, Jed, her mother, and her father. She wanted to be alone with this beautiful, shining thing and to discover its mysteries by herself. Jed might start showing her how everything worked, and she wouldn't be able to stop him.

"Barney looks so forlorn." Her mother, still in her morning robe, waved to the horse. A vague, bewildered look was on her face, as if to say, "Why is everyone out here before breakfast looking at a car?"

"He's not forlorn at all," Dina said quickly. "He knows I still love him."

"The registration's in the glove compartment," Mr. Stacey said, his red face beaming. Not every man could give his daughter a new sports car for her seventeenth birthday.

"Come on, let me take you for a ride." Jed's handsome, eager face was beckoning, causing a tumult of uncertainty to wash over Dina, shivering now in the cold Connecticut spring morning. How could she say no to Jed, who gave as easily as he took, but so seldom had anything that she wanted? Was he remembering all the rides he'd offered her on his motor scooter when it was new? The fact that after the first one she'd refused didn't matter; he'd asked her just the same. She hadn't been afraid—speeding up and down the hills with her hair flying, clinging to Jed, loving it—but the thought had occurred to her that if she said no, perhaps he would take the hint. Her experiment, however, had not worked. He still walked off with all her favorite records when he left for college, promising her extravagantly that he'd mail them back or bring them back at Thanksgiving, well, Christmas at the latest. As of this day they were still someplace in a dorm in Massachusetts, and she had no idea if they were still intact.

Nevertheless, she couldn't fight with Jed and tell him not to do something any more than she could say she wanted to have the first ride in her own new car by herself. Dina's family didn't say such things. They talked around things, distracted by non sequiturs (her mother) or trivia (her father), ducking behind words like *well, maybe, perhaps,* or *mmmm, we'll see,* but never coming right out with something essential and important that she might want to hear. Talk about feelings was *verboten.*

No one had said to her, "We are giving you this beautiful car because you are a wonderful girl and this present is a mark of our love and our trust." Oh no, that attitude would be too hearts and flowers for her parents. The car was bought for other *practical* reasons: "If you get a summer job, you'll have transportation." "You won't be taking your mother's car when she needs it." "When the other

11

cars have to go in for servicing, having a third car in the family will be handy."

Why did they have to weigh down a glorious present with all their garbage? Dina's car. She felt like someone wearing the wrong dress to a party, abashed by her gaucheness, wishing someone would hug her and say, "Go take your car for a ride, we understand." A memory knocked. The time she was nine and had sent Jed a valentine. Imagine sending one's own brother a valentine. Such sentimentality. Her mother's low laugh was the same then as it was now, before she asked, "Why are we all standing out here in the cold staring at a car? We look like a ridiculous ad. Let's go in and have breakfast."

"Yes, let's go in for breakfast," Dina said, grabbing at the suggestion, grateful for an excuse not to answer Jed's invitation to go for a ride in her own car.

Sunday morning breakfast, like every other unimportant event at the Staceys', was conducted with decorum. Everyone had to sit down at the table together and be served by Hattie the cook, as if pretending to be at a leisurely dinner party.

"My popovers are getting cold," Hattie grumbled.

"It's Dina's birthday," Mrs. Stacey announced, as if she had just remembered herself. A small-boned, plump woman with a vague undefined expression on her face,

Mrs. Stacey was constantly bewildered and surprised by the vagaries of those around her, and she drifted through life immersed in a cloud of memories of her own beaux and her own youth. Dina and Jed were wearisome mysteries to her. "You're talking too loud. . . . Do sit quietly. . . . Don't jump around so. . . . Do leave me alone!" She preferred her own befogged quietude. Buried under the mass of disappointments she had accumulated, she had long ago ceased to wonder why life had not turned out to be as bright and shining as her debutante days had promised. "Can't you do something with your hair?" she asked her daughter.

"What's the matter with my hair?" Dina ran her fingers through the tangled mass of blond hair that fell below her shoulders. "I like it this way," she said, answering her mother's unasked question of why she hadn't brushed and combed it.

"I think I'll have a glass of sherry to celebrate Dina's birthday," Mrs. Stacey said abruptly, halfway through her eggs and chicken livers.

Dina and Jed exchanged glances, Dina pulling her eyes away hurriedly, not wanting to meet Jed's fully. They both knew what the next move would be.

To no one's surprise, Mr. Stacey jumped up to the small sideboard that served as a bar. "Great idea. I'll join you with a little drink myself." He poured Mrs. Stacey a glass of sherry and mixed a highball for himself. "We'll drink to Dina," he said jovially.

Dina felt herself shrink inside. That toast was the end of them for the day, she thought morosely—and yet, was it? She had seen them start drinking in the morning before, yet manage to keep up their semblance of normal functioning, her mother no more or less vague, her father as convivial and hail-fellow-well-met as ever. Their drinking was a much discussed point of disagreement between her and Jed.

"Of course, they're alcoholic," was Jed's resigned argument. "You just don't want to see it."

"Certainly I don't," Dina would say. To herself she thought, Who wants to think of her parents as alcoholics? Sometimes she suspected Jed rather enjoyed the idea. An alcoholic to Dina was someone who lived like a bum, like the men she had seen a few times down on the Bowery in New York City. They were unshaven, asked for handouts, wore soiled, torn clothes. . . . Nice people might drink too much sometimes, but they couldn't be alcoholics. After all her father commuted every day to his job in an advertising agency in New York, and he earned a good salary; she didn't believe the firm would keep him on the job if he were an alcoholic. And her mother—well, her mother didn't have to do very much, that was true. Still, her mother seemed very little different when she was drinking from when she wasn't. Actually sometimes a few drinks made her seem for a while more attentive and less vague.

"And what are you going to do today to celebrate?" Mrs. Stacey asked Dina, the sherry making her eyes brighter.

"Go out in my car," Dina said with a laugh. "I guess I'll go over to see Stan."

Her mother frowned. "Oh, that Stan. Tom Hennessey's having a terrible time with him."

"Oh, that Tom Hennessey! He's a clump!"

Jed laughed. "Who gave him that name? It suits him perfectly."

"Stan did," Dina told him.

"You are both very rude. Tom Hennessey is a good friend of your father's, isn't he, Paul?" Laura Stacey turned to her husband. He nodded his head in agreement, but he was beginning to sulk about its being too cold to play golf.

"Mr. Hennessey is doing everything he can for Stan, but that boy is impossible." Mrs. Stacey punctuated her remark by draining her sherry and refilling her glass.

"Stan wishes he'd leave him alone," Dina murmured. Stan Palmer was Dina's boyfriend, and Mr. Hennessey was his newly acquired stepfather. Stan's own father, divorced from his mother, had gone off to Saudi Arabia several years earlier, and Stan had barely heard from him since.

The conversation drifted off. Drifting, drifting. Things always drifted in their household, Dina thought. There was never a period, a conclusion, not even a good fight. Sometimes she yearned to have something precise told to her. Instead of the usual, "Don't come in late," why didn't they name a time and say "Be home by twelve o'clock or one o'clock or two o'clock"? Maybe she'd hate the discipline and complain like her friend Helen Colby, who always had to dash home, but even hating it would be better than living in all this wishy-washiness. Except for rare weekends like this one, when her birthday had brought him home, Jed was away at college. Then there was no one to talk to, no one who finished a sentence or a thought, no one who paid attention.

And Dina liked attention. Attention and excitement. "On stage," her mother described her. "You're always so dramatic." She liked to live that way, on the outermost edge of feeling. "I want to feel everything there is to feel," she said to Helen. "Experience everything. I don't want to miss any emotion."

"But some of them are unpleasant," Helen said.

"I don't care." Dina would toss her head with its tangled mass of hair. "I know that. But tragedy is as important as happiness. You have to feel both. I'm not afraid of being unhappy; tragic women are interesting."

16

Dina even found herself being jealous of the fights that Helen had at home. Helen's family screamed at each other, little caring who was around to watch, and as likely as not Dina was. They hurled words about, slammed doors, and sometimes broke crockery. Helen would end up ashamed and tearstained, apologizing to Dina, but Dina was aglow with excitement. "They're wonderful, you too, all of you. You say what you think, and you're all so opinionated. What if you do scream and disagree, you shouldn't be upset. You're really living." Dina thought of the sham in her own house, where everyone was pretending; even she pretended that things were different from what they really were.

After breakfast, upstairs in her room, Dina looked at the array of stuffed animals on her window seat. The large panda with his big black-rimmed beady eyes was the last acquisition. Stan had won him for her at a carnival and as usual she loved him the best, because he was the newest. "Aren't you going to get rid of those things?" Jed had asked. "Seventeen's a little old for playing with toys."

"Oh, I don't play with them," Dina had told him, sweeping the panda up in her arms. "But I couldn't dream of throwing them away."

"You're going to have to someday," Jed said kindly.

"Why? I can take them with me when I get married. I'll save them for my children," Dina had told him, hugging the panda to her. He was soft and warm and cuddly, and although she wouldn't ever tell Jed, she sometimes took him to bed with her. The night became less lonesome.

Looking out the window, she saw her horse Barney and felt the same kind of warm, almost painful, nostalgia as when she hugged the panda. Perhaps the fuzzy animal or the horse with the large sad eyes understood all the different feelings that she had. They seemed to respond as if to say, "We've felt that way too. We know what it's like. . . ."

In a way this birthday was more important than her sixteenth. Seventeen. The word had a different sound to it. The sound of motion. Flying through the night, dancing, high heels tapping, extreme clothes, the sound of music, Stan's guitar, driving her car fast, fast, faster. . . .

But she was also leaving something behind. Was she being silly holding on to her beloved stuffed animals? Did Barney truly have a forlorn look about him? Quickly Dina ran downstairs and outside to Barney throwing her arms around the horse's neck and rubbing her own nose against his smooth brown one. He smelled good, really better than a car, with his mixed odor of woods and stable and leather. "Barney, Barney darling, I'll never stop loving you. Never." The horse stood patiently accepting her embraces and let out a low whinny in response. "Don't be sad, Barney. Even if I have a car we'll still go for rides in the woods. I promise you we will." The horse looked at her with his big, soft

18

brown eyes, and then shook his head. Dina laughed because he seemed to be answering her.

A minute later Dina was in the kitchen. "Hattie, quick, quick. I must have some apples. Where are the apples?"

Hattie looked up placidly from the dough she was kneading. "That's no way for you to talk. I taught you better manners myself. We haven't any apples."

"No apples? I never heard of a house without apples. That's ridiculous. Why not?"

"They're mealy this time of year. That's why."

"Then I suppose I'll have to give Barney sugar. Don't be angry with me, Hattie darling. It's my birthday." She kissed Hattie's cheek in passing and grabbed a handful of sugar lumps.

"Someday you're going to get into trouble, Miss Dina, real trouble," Hattie called after her, "with your flighty ways."

Dina fed Barney his lumps of sugar, patting his head lovingly. She wanted everyone and everything to be happy —Barney, the new car, her stuffed animals, Jed, her parents, Hattie, Stan, Helen—and *she* wanted to make them happy, to make sure, to arrange, to pour out her love.

"Come on, Jed," she called. "Let's go for a ride." She was ready to forget her momentary resentment earlier in the morning. Jed was leaving later in the day, and she wanted to share her first ride with him.

"You want to drive, don't you?" Generously Dina slid into the passenger seat of the two-seater car. She was tall, like Jed, but more narrowly built, hipless, and as flat as he. She had to crouch awkwardly to get into the car, but once inside she felt that it fit her like a second skin. "Isn't it divine?"

Jed drove the car smoothly out of the driveway. "Runs like a dream."

Dina threw her head back, loving the way the wind caught her hair. "Let's see how fast she'll go."

Jed stepped on the accelerator, and the little red car sped around the curves of the country road. Dina was too ecstatic to talk, too happy to feel the cold of the March wind pulling at her heavy sweater. The day was bright with little lacey clouds occasionally blotting out the sun. The rhythm of the car was her rhythm, the purr of the motor was the same as her heartbeat, the turning of the wheels kept pace with her spinning thoughts and emotions. "I'm a car-crazy kid," she sighed with joy.

"Let's go to Stan's," Dina said just in time for Jed to swing sharply into a side road. "Oh, watch her take those curves." Dina had to clutch the side of the car to keep her balance.

"My scooter does them better," Jed said.

They could hear the music of Stan's group as they drove up to his house. Dina tooted the horn.

20

Stan and the boys came trooping out. The four of them were dressed alike in black slim chinos, black boots on high square heels, and black jackets with the word *Beasts* embroidered in white on the back. Stan's thick, dark hair was almost down to his shoulders. The other three—Harry, Mike, and Bob—had hair that was only slightly shorter. The four of them could have passed as Elizabethan troubadors.

They had been playing together in a combo for the past couple of years. Stan, the leader, Mike, and Bob played electric guitars, Stan playing the bass, and Harry was the drummer. They performed wherever they could get engagements—at school dances, some night spots, occasionally at private parties. Now for the first time they had a regular date every Friday and Saturday night at the Ink Spot, a local hangout for the teen-agers.

"It's neat," Stan said, observing the car. His long, moody face scowled against the sun. He looked perpetually sleepy, and a good deal of the time he was. "I'm a night person," Stan described himself. "There's always something better to do than going to bed."

"Cute little toy," Mike commented. He was tall and graceful, with a kind of easy elegance that the rough clothes couldn't hide. The dreamy one of the quartet, he sometimes forgot the beat, often showed up late, and once in a while disappeared altogether.

"Come on, I'll take you for a ride," Dina suggested. Harry was ready to climb into the car. He was a small, tight bundle of energy—volatile, excitable, the mad drummer, they sometimes called him. When he played he whipped himself up into a frenzy, the sweat pouring down his face. One would think he was going to die of exhaustion when he finished a number, but he picked himself right up and was ready to start all over again.

"We can't now. We're rehearsing," Stan said. Stan wrote many of the songs the boys played. His sleepy face concealed a strong, bright mind, and when action was needed, he was ready.

"You can rehearse later," Dina coaxed.

"The little manager," Stan remarked.

"Don't be mean. It's my birthday," Dina flashed back at him. They were always at each other. The teasing was part of the game they played between them.

"Oh, yeah. Happy birthday," Stan said with a grin. Dina knew him well enough to understand that his happy birthday to her would come when they were alone.

"Come on," Harry said. "Bob, you and I can go for a ride. Mike and Stan have to work out their end of our new number anyway." Bob was the youngest of the group, but also the most serious about following a professional career in music.

"Everybody can't go," Jed said.

"Oh, sure we can. I'll drive this time." Dina exchanged seats with Jed. "You and Harry can crowd in, and Bob can sit on both your laps."

"You'll get a ticket," Stan warned.

"Who's going to give me a ticket on Sunday? Old Pop Wise is home taking his nap." Dina mentioned the local constable.

"I suppose you've never heard of state troopers?"

"Who are they?" Dina flashed him a sweet smile, and then she was careening out of the driveway. The load was too big for the small car. Dina felt the car's sluggishness as soon as she was out on the road, but she was not one to give up easily.

"Why didn't you get a four seater?" Bob gasped, hanging on with one hand on the door, and the other grasping Jed or Harry indiscriminately.

"You're not light, man," Harry commented.

They were rounding a curve when they heard a siren behind them. "Girl, I think we're being followed," Jed said. "You'd better pull over."

"You're just imagining things," Dina said unconvincingly. But glancing into the mirror, she saw a tan state police car behind her. There was no mistaking the purpose of the police officer behind the wheel.

Dina stopped at the side of the road as the police car drove up alongside of her.

"Let me see your registration." The officer was young and brisk.

Jed took the registration out of the glove compartment and handed it to the officer across Dina.

"Your license, please." Dina dug into the back pocket of her jeans, pulled out a scrubby wallet, and took her license out of it. Having it with her was pure luck as she often flew out of the house without it.

"You the owner of this car?"

"Yes sir." Dina had already managed to get some tears in her eyes.

"Don't you know it's against the law to carry more than one passenger in a two-seater car?" His blue eyes were a shade sympathetic.

Dina let the tears roll down her cheeks. "I didn't know . . . oh, I feel awful. It's my birthday, and I just got this car for a present. It's the first time I'm driving it. I was so excited about it that I wanted to take my brother and a couple of friends with me to try it out. I don't know what my father will say. I didn't know it was against the law."

"Well, you know now. I'll let you go this time with a warning, considering you just got the car. But remember, you can carry only one person. And you'd better take those curves a little slower too. You go on, take your friends home. Don't drive around this way." The officer didn't smile, but Dina thought that maybe inside he was.

24

"Oh, thank you. Thank you so much. I promise I'll never overload the car again. You've no idea how much I appreciate your giving me a chance. . . ." There was a little sob in her throat. "Thank you, officer."

Dina drove very carefully and sedately. No one spoke until they were out of sight of the police car.

"You should have been an actress," Harry said.

"But I did feel awful," Dina said.

"How did you manage to pull that crying gag?" Bob asked.

"You don't know my sister," Jed told them. "She was really crying. She can dramatize anything in a minute flat."

"But I wasn't putting on an act," Dina insisted. And she spoke truthfully. Her crying had been real, not faked. Dina could pull out any emotion that she needed at an instant's notice. The whole spectrum was there, ready to come to the surface to fit the wide range of her moods and needs.

When they got out of the car back at Stan's house, Dina said to Jed in an aside. "I don't think it makes any sense to worry Dad. Let's not mention the cop bit to him."

Jed looked at his sister in amazement. "I won't tell him. I'm not an idiot. But you never cease to astonish me. So *you're* protecting Dad by not telling him. That's a laugh."

Dina merely grinned and walked over to Stan with her

arms outstretched. "Give me my birthday kiss," she said gaily.

Later that afternoon Stan and his group came over to Dina's to play the new song Stan had written for her. The Hennesseys and a few other friends were with Mr. and Mrs. Stacey. All the grown-up eyes stared their criticism: Why don't they cut their hair? Why do they have to wear black? Why do they like such high heels on their boots? Why don't they leave us alone, Dina thought, wordlessly too.

Down in the basement, Stan was singing his song. "A girl in a car . . . picks up a boy . . . before they get to the edge of the town . . . with his eyes he's put a knife in her heart . . . the twist of it hurts as she drives on alone. . . ."

"It's beautiful. Makes me cry." Dina had tears in her eyes again.

"Sad song. Sad, sad," Harry said.

"Sad world. Full of clumps," Stan said. "The whole world, nothing but clumps."

"Should blow it up and start all over again," Mike said.

"Not yet. Wait a hundred years. Got a lot to do." Bob strummed on his guitar.

"Not such a bad world. Has beautiful cars in it. Little red ones that go hoppity hoppity hop," Dina said. "Great affluent society."

"Yeah, man, great affluent society." Stan was singing the words to music. "Man, oh man, that great affluent society. Met a boy, he had no legs, but he drove a beautiful shiny red car; met a man, he had no arms, but he drove a beautiful shiny red car; met a girl, she had no hair, but she drove a beautiful shiny red car. . . ."

"Got something there, boy." Bob took up the notes on his guitar.

"Stop it. I can't stand it. Makes me weep, weep," Dina cried out.

"Met a girl with tear gas in her eyes, but she was driving a beautiful shiny red car," Stan answered her with his song.

"Do you kids have to make all this noise?" Tom Hennessey was in the doorway, his red face and little eyes making him look like an angry beetle.

A sudden silence. How dare he? He's not even in his own house. What would happen if Stan hit him? If he simply walked up to him and punched him in that fat, red face?

"Didn't think we were making noise, sir. Just playing music." Stan's voice was quiet. Mr. Hennessey's floral shirt voluminous on his big frame, too bright and gay for his anger. The electric currents between those two shimmering in the room, a dark thundercloud, frightening Dina.

"Don't sir me. If you played music, it wouldn't be so bad. But this stuff you moan about, it's . . . it's indecent." He

27

faltered on the word as if he'd found a friend. "Indecent, just indecent. When I was a kid we sang nice songs, nice wholesome songs."

"Yes, sir. Oh, I'm sorry," Stan added quickly.

They stared at each other. The big man suddenly helpless, defeated against five solemn faces—a large, floral balloon punctured. "Keep the noise down," he muttered, and stumped back upstairs.

"Come on, Dina. Let's go for a ride in your new car," Stan said abruptly. "You fellas take my car."

Dusk was softening the landscape, giving pale spring colors to the wintry bleakness. "I'll drive," Stan spoke authoritatively.

Someplace there was tenderness in him. Dina knew she could find it if she probed enough, but not yet. She hadn't dared to come that close to him. "He has a spiked fence around him," Helen said. "You'll get hurt."

"I'm not afraid. I'll take my chances." Helen never understood that she didn't mind getting hurt. That experience, too, was part of living and loving, and she was sure Stan would never hurt her. Sometimes he had no manners, sometimes his quiet shut her out, but when he brushed the hair away from her eyes his hands were gentle and his eyes could grow soft.

"How can you take them?" Stan's sleepy eyes had little daggers in them.

"What's the use?" Dina stretched her legs down into the car, careful not to touch him. She knew he was referring to their parents. "We're stuck with them. No exit. I leave them alone. They leave me alone."

"They never leave me alone. Always at me. Never let up for a minute. We'll escape. We'll go to Samoa." He stepped on the gas. Their private joke, Samoa was a little cove on the beach they considered their own.

It was bleak now with the March winds blowing whitecaps on the water and waves breaking over the rocks. They sat silently in the car.

"And how are you?" Stan turned to her.

"I'm a girl who never combs her hair."

"I'm a boy who never cuts his."

"We're no good. We're rotten through and through."

"We'll come to no good."

"We'll never own a ranch house."

"We'll never meet the mortgage payments."

"Our children will be dirty little brats. They'll never clean their teeth."

They laughed. They laughed and laughed until Dina said, "Stop, it gives me a pain in my side."

"I like you, girl," Stan said.

"I like you too."

2

Helen looked like a snake with her short, sleek hair and her sphinxlike face. A snake with darting, knowing eyes. "What's going to happen that's so big at the Ink Spot tonight?" she asked Dina, not taking her eyes away from her own reflection in the mirror as she held up one earring after another to study the effect. It was Saturday afternoon, and the two girls were at Helen's house, languidly gossiping and more or less getting themselves ready for the usual Saturday-night dance.

"The boys have some new songs, and Stan said that a bunch of kids were coming over from Allentown. It should be fun." Dina took the pink polish off her nails and put on some of Helen's pearly white. She held out her fingers to admire their divinely unhealthy appearance.

"What's so great about Allentown?" Helen queried, trying to decide between a pair of long pearl earrings and a pair of old garnet ones. "Probably be a bunch of townies, and wild ones at that." *Townies* was the name generally given to the girls and boys whose parents worked in the nearby factories and stores and did not commute to New York City.

Dina raised her eyebrows in a frown. "I hate that word *townies*. Makes the kids sound like something inferior, which they aren't. I'm surprised at you, Helen. And as soon as someone says *townies*, the next word is bound to be *wild*. They're no wilder than we are. Maybe less so."

Helen looked at Dina and laughed. "You do get excited, don't you? I'm not trying to insult anyone."

"I know you're not," Dina said apologetically. "But there is a kind of snobbery that exists, and I don't like it. Just because our parents don't mix is no reason we shouldn't."

"Hurrah for the working class!" Helen said mockingly. "I suspect their parents would find our parents a big bore," she added more seriously.

"Who would find us a bore?" Helen's mother burst into

the room. She was wearing a purple smocked dress, her bare feet in sandals. Without waiting for an answer, she thrust a question at Helen. "Is that passage, 'It is a tale told by an idiot, full of sound and fury' from *Macbeth* or *Hamlet?*"

"I've asked you a million times to please knock before you come into my room." Helen's mouth puckered up with annoyance.

"She's telling me what to do!" Mrs. Colby said to Dina. "Everything's upside down in this house." Dina was afraid they were going to get into one of their fights and she wasn't in the mood for a fight. "Just answer my question. I'm trying to meet a deadline." Mrs. Colby wrote mysteries that were published in paperbacks.

"It's from *Macbeth*," Helen said sulkily. "I don't know what you're going to do when I get married. You never look anything up."

"Why should I when I have such a smart daughter?" Mrs. Colby said with a quick smile, and was out of the room as abruptly as she had come in.

"You should be flattered," Dina said in answer to the grimace Helen made. She liked Mrs. Colby, with her Greenwich Village clothes, her bangles and long earrings, and her unpredictable ways, screaming at Helen one minute and treating her like an equal the next.

"Come on," Dina suggested, seeing that Helen was upset. "Let's go for a ride."

The two girls were almost out the door when Mrs. Colby's shrill voice called out from her study. "You're not going anywhere, Helen. I have to finish my chapter, and you have to make supper."

"There's plenty of time. I'll be back in half an hour."

"I know your half hours. You are not to leave this house. You hear me?"

"I could hear you if I were a mile away." Helen was pushing Dina to go ahead, but Mrs. Colby was out of her room and facing them. "Don't you talk fresh to me, Helen Colby. I work too hard to take any lip from you."

"I wasn't being fresh. You're the one who's rude, screaming at me this way when I have a guest. How would you like it if I did the same thing when you had company?"

"As if you haven't." Mrs. Colby's earrings and bangles were making little tinkling noises. "Excuse me, Dina, but Helen cannot go out with you now." Quite gently she pushed Dina through the front door and closed it shut.

Dina could hear the two of them inside, both their voices getting shrill and loud. She slipped into her little red car gratefully. Escape, escape. Stan's catchword.

The car was her escape. How had she ever lived without it? Where had she gone to hide, to be alone, to think, to be free? She snuggled down into the seat, feeling as if the car were actually wrapping itself around her the way she used to pull her *gogie* around her. *Gogie* was the baby name she had given the torn, soiled blanket she had trailed behind her everyplace she went.

She still remembered the day her parents had taken her *gogie* away from her. It was either her fourth of fifth birthday—that part she didn't remember—and there was a party. Colored paper ribbons coming down from the chandelier, favors, paper hats, putting the tail on the donkey, and a treasure hunt. Lovely presents to open as each small guest arrived. She had worn a white dress with a blue sash, and her mother had put a big blue ribbon on top of her straight hair. Then, when the huge birthday cake had been brought in on a silver tray, with much fanfare, the candles lighted, and everyone at the table started to sing "Happy Birthday," the party had all become too much for her. She remembered clearly a sense of panic, of wanting to cry, and of wishing desperately that the children would not sing that song. She had run away from the table, up to her room, and wrapped her *gogie* around her.

Her mother had come up after her. "You mustn't leave your guests. That's not a nice thing to do."

"I don't want them to sing," Dina had sobbed.

"What a silly girl you are. They're only wishing you a happy birthday. Come on downstairs."

Still whimpering, Dina had started to follow her mother out of her room, trailing her *gogie* after her.

"Not with that horrid dirty thing. You're too big a girl for that now. This is a good time to get rid of that awful rag once and for all." To Dina's horror, her mother had snatched the blanket from her and marched her downstairs. There she handed it over to Hattie. "Burn this. I never want to see it again."

Dina had put on a pretty good show in front of her friends, but she had hated the party after that moment. She'd have preferred her *gogie* to all the presents in the world. And when she went to bed that night she was inconsolable. Everyone had tried to quiet her down: her mother, her father, Hattie, and even Jed. Being told that she was a big girl made her cry the harder. If this unhappiness was growing up, she didn't want to change.

Her hand touched the side of the car. It was cold and hard and unyielding, but it comforted her. Whenever she felt a surge of loneliness she wanted something or someone to cling to. Her hands moved to the steering wheel, and she gripped it tightly. The car was her friend, her refuge, her consolation.

In spite of Helen's remarks to Dina earlier that afternoon, the two groups from their town and from Allentown usually mixed well. A friendly rivalry had existed for years on the ball field and on the basketball court. However, a recent editorial in the local newspaper had raised the subject of undesirable elements coming to the Ink Spot, and it alarmed the parents. Everyone knew the writer was referring to the Allentown kids, and the issue had provoked unresolved but angry discussions in many households between the teen-agers and their parents. The teen-agers had stoutly defended their peers, but the discussion itself had unavoidably created tension in the community over the Ink Spot.

Dina, Helen, and Helen's boyfriend Timmy Kavanec, sitting at a table together, could feel an electric current of excitement in the air. The room was filled with their own crowd, and Dina wondered how the Allentown group would find space when they arrived. Once again the group began discussing the newspaper editorial.

"It's ridiculous," Dina said impatiently. "There's no problem. The Allentown kids aren't any different from us. I'm sick of the hypocrisy and snobbery in this town."

"The grown-ups are afraid we're going to learn about s-e-x from them," Timmy said in a mocking stage whisper.

"Sometimes I think they're just waiting for us to do something wrong, hoping we will in a way, so they can pounce on us," Dina said rebelliously. She sensed a hostility to teen-agers in the community, as if many people were taking out their own disappointments and frustrations on the kids. They talk around everything, she thought, making a mystery out of sex and anything else that has to do with reality.

Even my own mother's never mentioned the word *sex* out loud!

"What's the joke, Dina?" Helen asked.

"I was thinking of my mother trying to educate me about sex. She would be hilarious. She'd say, now my dear, you, know, but well, maybe you don't, but perhaps, although of course . . . but everyone does know and does do it, but you are so awfully young, dear. Now why don't you run along and comb your hair?" Her voice had exactly imitated her mother's hesitation and tone, causing the others to laugh gaily.

The combo finished playing then, and Stan joined them at the table. "That was a good number," Dina said approvingly. "When are your friends coming?"

"Anytime now." Stan looked around the room. "There'll be quite a crowd. Hope no one makes a fuss." There was an apprehensive note in his voice.

"Like who?" Dina asked.

"Like some of the nuts in this town who have it in for us and this place. I don't know what they think goes on here. They've got us living on dope, LSD, and having wild orgies. We're a real evil bunch. Better call out the riot squad."

37

The four looked around the room and laughed. The noise from the jukebox, which went on as soon as the boys stopped playing, was loud, and many couples were dancing. But the worst that could be said was that the room was very noisy and the dancing was, to say the least, vigorous. "But," as Stan said, "they don't expect us to waltz, do they?"

When a few minutes later, the door opened and the Allentown crowd came in, Dina felt the tension in the air deepen. Admittedly, the boys were older—some of them looked more like men than boys—and they appeared tougher. The girls too looked older, for they were more dressed up than Dina and her friends were. Frank, the apparent leader of the group, came over and greeted Stan, and Dina noticed that some of the young men had brought their guitars with them. Stan asked several couples to double up at the tables so that there would be room for the newcomers.

When Stan and the combo started playing again, Frank and two others joined them on their guitars, and another boy added his drums to Harry's. The music started out comparatively softly, but it built up to a quicker and quicker tempo and became louder and louder. The dance floor was jammed with swaying couples.

"This place is really swinging," Dina remarked.

But the atmosphere was mild compared to what was to

come. The music became wilder and wilder, the boys playing as if each of the two groups were competing to see who could produce the louder, faster music. And the dancing couples kept up with them. Helen and Timmy left Dina at the table while they went to join the dancing.

One of the boys from the Allentown group, seeing her sitting alone, came over and asked her if she wanted to dance. Dina agreed readily.

They faced each other silently on the crowded floor, their bodies not touching, and immediately became part of a writhing, wriggling mass of human beings. They danced away from each other and toward each other, never once missing the beat of the fast rhythm, their arms, legs, their entire beings in constant motion. Although they danced as partners, each one daring the other on with wilder movements, they also danced alone, as if manipulated by an unseen mad puppeteer, who was making them go faster and faster.

"It's wild, isn't it?" Dina said to her partner, dancing with all the abandon she had, catching Stan's eye when she could, but letting herself go completely to the furious music.

"We'll shake the building down," the young man said with a grin. Dina wondered for a moment if he couldn't be right as she thought she felt the floor tremble beneath them.

"Let's go!" he cried. Dina moved back, still facing him, colliding with other dancers, her eyes never leaving his. She was breathless with the movement and the excitement, the music pounding away in her ears.

"It's the greatest," she said. And she felt great. Everyone was having a marvelous time. Who came from Allentown and who came from home didn't matter anymore. Everyone was caught up in the same exuberant freedom of the dancing, the same excitement of the fast music. The drummers and guitarists continued to play furiously, sweat pouring off their faces, their long hair streaming. The dance was one to end all dances; there would never be anything like it again.

I don't even know this boy's name, Dina thought, and I will probably never see him again, but she felt a camaraderie with him, as she did with everyone else on the floor and with the musicians. They were all bound up together, having one smashing, sensational experience that was theirs and theirs alone; they were in a world of their own, where only the music and the rhythm mattered, and everyone and everything else was excluded. The parents would never understand, Dina thought.

"Here we go," the boy said, and Dina backed away from him again, every muscle in her body moving, vibrating to the music. There was no stopping her; she was caught up in a cloud of her own. She lost her partner, and then a strange boy was facing her. Soon she lost him too. She was a bundle of motion, her eyes closed, swaying from head to toe, when suddenly a strong hand grabbed her wrist. A stern voice belonging to someone tall was saying, "Dina, behave yourself."

Dina looked up into Tom Hennessey's eyes. If she'd seen the devil himself standing there, she couldn't have been more surprised. Apparently he had just entered the door together with Mr. Pratt, the owner of the Ink Spot.

Dina pulled her arm away from him. "I was only dancing," she said angrily.

"I don't call this dancing." Mr. Hennessey was looking at the pulsating room with disgust. "It's disgraceful . . . immoral. . . ."

"It's nothing of the kind," Dina said vehemently. "This is the way we dance. There's nothing wrong with it."

"We'll see about that," Mr. Hennessey muttered. They stood glaring at each other, until Dina turned away. But the spell had been broken, and she returned to her table instead of to the dance floor. Mr. Hennessey and Mr. Pratt remained talking for a few minutes and then left. Dina had seen Stan glance over and knew that he had noticed his stepfather there. She could tell by his face that he was furious.

41

As soon as the music stopped Stan came over to Dina's table. "What did my old man have to say?" he asked. Dina told him the extent of their brief conversation.

"He's up to something," Stan said. "He's looking for some excuse to get this place closed and to break up the Beasts. But he's got another think coming. We'll keep on playing no matter what." Stan spoke in his usual quiet voice, but Dina knew he was boiling.

"Can't we do something? Can't we stop them?" Dina had seen something that she didn't like in Mr. Hennessey's face. The place was loud and noisy, and the dancing was wild—no one could deny those facts. Yet Mr. Hennessey had invented a horrid and nasty scene that didn't exist, had created something in his own mind that made Dina bristle with indignation.

"There's nothing to do," Stan said. "Let's just wait and see what happens."

"They probably came because they heard the Allentown crowd would be here," Timmy suggested.

"I'm glad they were," Dina said. "There's no reason why they shouldn't come here; we're not exclusive."

The conversation drifted off to other things until the music started again. The night was one to remember. Dina didn't miss a dance, and by the end of the evening she was exhausted.

Later that night, parked at Samoa with Stan, she leaned

42

her head against his arm and looked up at the sky. "It was a beautiful night. There was something marvelous and exciting about it, the way everyone became one person. A teen-ager. Your stepfather was the only sour note. What does he have against us?"

"Who knows? He thinks we need more discipline and that our life is too easy. But his father probably said the same about him. He says we're wild." Stan pulled her to him. "I'm wild about you." He kissed her hard on the lips.

"What would you do if they closed the Ink Spot?" Dina asked, sitting up and facing him.

Stan shrugged. "Get a job someplace else."

"I wouldn't take his interference sitting down. I'd put up a fight." Her wide-set, slanted blue eyes were blazing. "You look more beautiful all the time," Stan remarked. "Do you love me, Dina?" he asked abruptly.

"How do I know? Sometimes I think I do, but I don't know what love is yet. Do you? Do you love me?"

"I think I do. But what do I know about love either?" He kissed her again. "This seems awful close to it," Stan said.

"I'm glad we're honest with each other." Dina stayed close to him. She couldn't get Mr. Hennessey's face out of her mind. He had looked at her, at them all, as if they were subhuman. She clung to Stan. She knew there were millions of kids in the world who had parents who cared and who loved them—perhaps her own parents cared and loved her too—but she felt alienated and alone. There was no older person in her life to whom she could really talk, and she was aware of the lack.

Was it love that she felt for Stan? Or was he the one person in the world she could count on? She didn't know and right now she didn't care. She was grateful that he was close and holding her tight.

3

Dina half listened to her parents' conversation at the dinner table. They never talked about anything important. She didn't know if they had heard about Saturday night at the Ink Spot. Tom Hennessey must have told them, if no one else did, but neither one of them said a word. They lived in another world. Right now they were discussing the rareness of the roast beef as if it were a matter of life and death. Had the roast been cooked five minutes too long?

Her father thought it had—"the blood should be running" —but her mother in her vague way wasn't sure. "Well, maybe, perhaps. . . ."

Sometimes she wanted to stand up and scream, "You have a teen-age daughter in the house. Don't you care anything about her besides whether or not she combs her hair? Don't you want to know her?"

"I think the story in the paper about the Ink Spot was perfectly horrid," she said, yearning for their attention.

Her mother looked puzzled and her father's face took on a blank expression, which meant that the subject bored him. "I don't know about that," her father spoke slowly. "We don't want a rowdy hangout in town."

"There's nothing rowdy about it," Dina said indignantly. "It's a perfectly good place, and we have a lot of fun there."

"Don't frown so, dear. It will give you wrinkles," Mrs. Stacey said.

"Oh, Mother!" Dina sighed out of frustration and exasperation. They could never make contact with each other about anything. She wanted to bang her fists against the wall that separated them, but there was nothing tangible to attack.

In school the next day the axe fell. Or so Dina and Stan and their friends in the senior class felt. A notice was given to every student in the high school. It started off with a

46

brief statement on a "looseness of deportment that was increasingly visible on the part of the student body" and "a carelessness in both manners and attire that demanded correction." As a first step in "bringing the students up to socially acceptable standards" new rules were to go into effect, beginning the following Monday, as to proper appearance in school. The girls were to dress in skirts (no slacks, blue jeans, or shorts), which could not be shorter than knee length. They could not wear tight sweaters, use heavy makeup, or indulge in elaborate hairdos. The boys were not to wear boots. Shirts with ties and a jacket or sweater were required, and no long hair or sideburns were permissible. They also could not wear shorts.

"It's the most ridiculous thing I ever heard of." Dina was outraged. "How stupid can they get? These rules are part of a campaign against teen-agers!"

"Of course they are," Helen agreed. "But you don't have to worry. You never wear jeans to school anyway." She adjusted her own snug pants and looked at Dina, whose tumbled hair was combed in anything but a studied coiffure and whose face was free of makeup except for pale eye shadow. That was Dina's style, which she considered far more chic than wearing bright lipstick and setting her hair.

"I've never liked jeans," Dina said, privately thinking they were passé, "and my mother won't let me wear slacks to school. I think she's absurd, but at least she's my mother.

I don't think the school has any business deciding what we should wear."

"You're right, they don't," Stan said. "If they think I'm going to cut my hair, they're crazy. I don't care so much about the clothes, but no one is going to tell me what to do with my hair."

"What will you do?" Dina asked, her eyes gleaming in anticipation of a battle.

"I won't cut it. That's all. It's simple."

"You'll never get away with it," Helen said.

"We'll see about that," Stan said darkly.

"You stick to your guns," Dina cheered him on enthusiastically.

Clothes and haircuts momentarily faded into the background on Friday night. Dina arrived at the Ink Spot in the little red car and found a group of teen-agers, including Stan and the boys, standing outside. The small, weather-beaten frame building, which stood by itself back from the highway, was boarded up. There was a big sign on the door, *Closed Until Further Notice.*

"Let's tear down the boards," Dina cried, springing out of the car. "This town is out of its mind."

"Don't touch anything." Stan put out his arms as if to protect the building. "You won't do any good, and I don't want them to get us for unlawfully breaking in or trespassing. We don't know who did this yet."

"What difference does it make who did it? The police, I suppose," Dina said. She was like a racehorse being held in check.

Stan shook his head. "The police would have to have a reason. Something unlawful would have had to happen. They can't go around just boarding up places."

"Let's go see the landlord," one of the boys suggested.

"Good idea." Stan got into the car with Dina, and the rest of the crowd piled into other cars and followed.

Dina drove quickly through the village to a neat red-brick house with a blue graveled walk in front. The house was blazing with lights. "Thank goodness, he's home," Dina remarked. She and Stan knocked on the front door while the other cars pulled to a stop. "The rest of you wait outside," Stan called out, as the door opened.

Mr. Pratt himself opened it. A man with tired lines on his face and weary eyes, he had obviously lost weight for his clothes hung loosely on him.

"Good evening, Mr. Pratt," Stan said, and the two of them stepped inside.

"I was expecting you," Mr. Pratt said in a tired voice.

"I should think so," Stan said tersely. "What's the idea of closing up the Ink Spot? You didn't even let us know."

The young people followed him into a stiffly furnished front room.

"Sit down, sit down." Mr. Pratt gestured to a brown sofa and some chairs. "I felt bad about that, but there wasn't time."

"What do you mean? What was all the rush about?" Stan asked.

"I figured up my accounts, and every week I was losing money. So I made up my mind to close down. That's the kind of man I am. I make up my mind to do something and I do it right away."

"You expect us to believe that? You must think we're an awful dumb bunch of kids." Stan looked up at Mr. Pratt sorrowfully. "We know that place was jammed every Friday and Saturday night. Maybe you weren't making a fortune, but you were doing all right. Someone made you close the place."

"Maybe someone did." Mr. Pratt lighted a cigarette uneasily. "Anyway, it's closed. So that's that. You kids will be better off at home."

"What a laugh," Stan murmured.

"It's outrageous." Dina sat on the edge of her chair, a long-legged machine ready to explode.

"Do you realize what you've done?" Stan demanded sternly of Mr. Pratt. "You've permitted a newspaper article and a few parents to intimidate you! They've pressured you into closing up the only place in town where teen-agers can have a little fun. My stepfather is at the bottom of this. I'm sure of it. You were there with him Saturday night. Did you see anything wrong?"

"It was overcrowded," Mr. Pratt said defensively.

"You said a minute ago you weren't making enough money," Stan retorted. "Make up your mind what your story is."

"It was overcrowded with the wrong kind of kids. I'm not running a place for hoodlums."

"That is unfair," Dina cried. "The Allentown kids aren't hoodlums. They're the same as we are. Some people are just looking for an excuse to close your place, and you've let them use this excuse."

Mr. Pratt looked more tired than ever. "It's my place, and I closed it," he said unconvincingly. However, Dina knew by the expression on his face that he had been persuaded by Mr. Hennessey, and probably others, and he was not going to change his mind for them.

Outside, the others wanted to know what happened, and Stan told them that they hadn't made much progress. "He says he decided to close the Ink Spot himself, but we know better. My stepfather was over there Saturday night with him, and I'm sure shutting down was his idea. He wants to break up the combo, but he's not going to stop us. We'll get other jobs."

"It's not just your stepfather," Helen said. "It's a conspiracy—the newspaper, the principal, most of the parents. They don't like the way we dress, the music we play, the way we dance, so they're clamping down."

"It's out and out war," Dina said with some glee.

"What are you going to do?" Dina asked Stan later, when they were alone, riding around in Dina's car.

"I don't know. When you come down to it, what can I do? Nothing, I guess," he said despondently.

"Don't be defeated so easily." Dina barely slowed down to take a curve. "Can't we all get together and do something? It's ridiculous for Mr. Pratt to close the Ink Spot."

"Of course, it is. But Mr. Pratt owns it, and if he wants to close it, who can stop him?"

"I think if all the teen-agers get together and put up a fight, we can accomplish something!" Dina was on the warpath.

"Who are we going to fight? You know we don't stand a chance."

"What are you going to do about the school clothes?" Dina asked.

"That's kid stuff. I don't care about the clothes, but I will not cut my hair. If the group is going to get playing jobs, we have to keep our hair long. That's all there is to it."

"I hope you stick to it," Dina said.

"You think I won't?" Stan gave her a sidelong glance.

"I don't know. I don't think you're a fighter."

"I'll fight if I think I have a chance of winning. And if it's important enough. But I won't fight for nothing, the way you will."

"It's a question of principle," Dina said firmly. "A person doesn't always know in advance if he's going to win or not."

"I haven't got the time for all this fighting," Stan said. "I just want my parents to leave me alone, and I want the group to play. If we can't play at the Ink Spot, we'll play someplace else."

Dina pulled the car to a stop at Samoa. She sat silently and made a move away from him as he tried to put his arm around her. "What's the matter? What are you mad about?"

Dina didn't answer for a few minutes. "I'm not mad," she murmured finally. Her feelings about Stan were ambivalent. She was crazy about him, she was sure of that, yet she wanted him to be more fiery, to get angry and indignant the way she did. His calmness infuriated her. There was no logic to her feelings, because she felt that he had more sense than she did. When he stayed calm he made her anger seem childish. Still, she wanted him to get worked up the way she did.

"You want me to be mad about the Ink Spot, don't you?" Stan said, knowing her well.

"I don't want you to take it lying down," Dina told him.

"Don't you see, baby, I'd do something if there was something to do. I don't believe in making useless motions."

"How do you know they're useless until you try?"

"I think them out. You want to thrash around whether you accomplish anything or not."

"Sometimes I want to shake you," Dina said.

"Go ahead if it'll make you feel better." Then he took her in his arms and kissed her. She resisted for a second or two and finally gave in to the warmth of his kisses. "I do love you, Dina," he said softly.

She lay back in his arms, but she didn't answer.

"You never say that you love me," Stan said unhappily.

"I can't say it until I'm sure. Most times I think I do, but other times I don't know. . . ."

"I can wait."

"Maybe that's the trouble. You're willing to wait," Dina said with a little laugh.

"But I am. I can't help it. I don't want to force you to say you love me or else. Where would that get me?"

"You're always so logical." One day, she vowed, she would break that calm of his. "How do you know that I wouldn't say that I love you if you made an issue of it?" She flashed him a wide smile and drew away teasingly.

"When you're ready, you'll say so."

Perhaps I never will, she thought, yet he would never let

me know if he were hurt or not. He would walk right away and never come back as soon as I told him I *didn't* love him. He has me dangling just as much as I have him, but the realization gave her little pleasure or satisfaction.

When Dina left Stan at his door, she didn't want to go home. There was more than a hint of spring in the air, and the narrow crescent moon looked like half a wedding band. She felt discontented and restless as if something was left unfinished. Suddenly she knew what it was.

Dina drove through the night, letting the car take the winding road as if it were part of her, until she reached the Ink Spot. Defiantly she pulled into the parking area with a skid against the gravel. She turned off the headlights and got out of the car. Her eyes unadjusted to the darkness, she could barely make out the words on the boarded-up building: *Closed Until Further Notice.*

It wasn't yet midnight, and on any other Friday night the place would be ablaze with lights, music, and dancing. The quietness was oppressive, and for a frightening moment she felt that adult eyes were leering at her from behind the trees, that warning fingers were being raised at her. But her wild notion had taken complete possession of her.

She knew it was wild, it made no sense, it was what Stan would call "feminine and emotional." But that's what I am, and I'm going to do it.

Quickly she walked to the edge of the gravel, and her eyes searched out a large stone, almost a rock. Dina picked it up and with all her might hurled it against the boarded-up façade of the building. Her strike hit. She heard glass shattering, and to her amazement the sound filled her with delight.

The act was useless. It accomplished nothing. Yet throwing the stone against the building made Dina feel as if she had accomplished something. The gesture is mine, my tiny cry against unfairness, against stupidity. So be it. *They* will know that someone objected, that someone made a protest.

Dina got back into the car and drove home slowly through the night, her thoughts on Stan. He would think me the fool, but the truth was that women broke crockery and cried alone. With a sense of loneliness she wondered if anyone in the world, male or female, would understand why she threw that rock.

4

Monday morning Dina stayed in bed later than usual. She had a plan, and part of it was to drive herself to school instead of taking the school bus. She would time her arrival for exactly nine o'clock when classes began. Carefully she picked out the clothes for her entrance. A boy's shirt, a skirt, but instead of her usual low-heeled shoes, a pair of sneakers. And in between her books, when she left her room, there was a neatly folded pair of blue jeans. Her father had left for work, and her mother didn't notice that she was using her car.

On the way to school Dina pulled into a side road, stripped off her skirt, and quickly slipped into her blue jeans. I didn't have to bother with all this secrecy, she thought bitterly. My mother wouldn't have known the difference! The school yard was cleared when Dina parked her car, and the nine o'clock bell ringing as she entered her classroom.

There was a gasp from the students when she walked into the room. The homeroom teacher, Mrs. Johnson, looked up from her desk, but didn't utter a sound. Dina took her seat silently, first having glanced quickly around the room to assure herself that the four Beasts had not cut their hair. The boys sat in a row, their hair untouched. The rest of the class looked so different that Dina had all she could do to keep from laughing aloud. All of them appeared self-conscious, as if they were in Sunday school. Ties, jackets, cropped hair, skirts, and blouses, those girls whose hair usually was piled high were now flatheaded. Sheep, sheep, no guts. Dina grimaced at Helen whose eyes burned bright with curiosity.

"The class will please stand up." Mrs. Johnson rapped her desk sharply. Her penetrating eyes went up and down the rows examining each boy and girl carefully. Those little eyes, set against pale lids, rested only a few seconds

58

longer on Dina and the boys. When she had finished her inspection, she called Dina and the four boys to the front of the room. Dina, with her long hair and jeans, almost looked like one of them until her finely outlined face and slanted blue eyes gave her away. A defiant face, warm and wild, on a head held high. Dare me, just dare me, her expression seemed to say. She didn't look at Mrs. Johnson, but at the class with no trace of a smile on her lips.

"How nice you all look today," Mrs. Johnson addressed the class, after telling them to be seated. "And what a pity that some cannot obey rules." She turned to the five. "You will report to Mr. Mann, please," she said, naming the principal.

Out in the hall the boys clustered around Dina. "Why did you do it?" Stan demanded. "You're a nut. You never wore jeans before."

"No one told me not to before. No one except my mother, and that's different. I don't like being told what to wear by teachers or principals."

"She's right," Harry said. "My folks were mad as hops. They said it's not the school's business."

"Not mine," Stan said. "They're all for it."

"My folks don't care one way or another," Mike said, "but I guess they'll go along with the school."

"Mine too," Bob echoed. "The parents aren't going to fight this policy, you can bet on that."

"I don't care about the parents. I'm going to." Dina's delicate, strong face was firmly set.

"I'm afraid you won't get very far. We can say we need to keep our hair long for work, but you have no real reason."

"My principle is my reason," Dina flashed back.

Stan shook his head. "Someday I'd like to see you get excited about something that really matters," he said with grudging admiration. "Not over whether you wear blue jeans to school!"

By this time they were in front of Mr. Mann's office. Harry knocked on the door, and it was promptly opened by the principal's secretary. The four boys and Dina filed in silently.

Mr. Mann's words to them were brief and to the point. He was not the least interested in Stan's plea that the group be made an exception because they needed long hair to get playing jobs, and he ended up by curtly telling them that all five were suspended from school until such time as they saw fit to comply with school rules.

"But—" Dina opened her mouth to protest.

"That is all. There is nothing to discuss, Miss Stacey." Mr. Mann dismissed them by picking up his telephone to make a call.

Dina's frustration was agonizing. She had been making up speeches to give him all weekend, and now he would not permit her to say a word!

"He's going to hear from my parents," Harry said, outside on the school grounds. "Am I glad to be out of that place!" he cried, his nervous, tense energy causing him to run down the driveway.

"You're not going to be so glad," Stan said gloomily, "when college boards come up."

"Yeah. What are we going to do about them?" Mike asked. They were all due to take their senior college board exams the following Saturday.

"I don't know. We'll have to think that one out," Stan said.

"You'll have to do some pretty fast thinking," Bob commented.

"Come on, fellas, don't be so gloomy." Harry rejoined them. "Let's stop at my house and tell my mother. Then we can practice."

"Practice for what? We've no place to play," Mike said.

"We can use this time to go around and see some of the clubs. Maybe we can line up some jobs," Stan said. He turned to Dina. "What are you going to do?"

She shrugged. "Go home, I guess." She felt let down and was still smarting from the rebuff of not being allowed to speak up. "Some way to teach us democracy," she said bitterly. "We're not supposed to say a word. What's that but autocratic rule? Why shouldn't we dress the way we want to? It's supposed to be a free country!"

"What's free about it?" Harry demanded. "Our taxes pay for Mann's salary, for the school, for everything. There's nothing free."

On that dismal note, the boys said good-bye. "See you later," Stan said to Dina.

Alone in her car, Dina followed the boys out of the school yard, but she didn't turn in the direction of home. She didn't want the least bit to see her mother or Hattie. Anger was welling up in her. She had hoped that something big and dramatic would happen, fiery words would be exchanged. But the meeting with Mr. Mann had been flat, cut-and-dried, and he had treated them as if they were naughty little children, instead of young adults with a point of view.

Dina stepped on the gas and drove. She turned into a country road and followed it up a long, steep hill. At the top she got out of the car and decided to take a walk. The woods now in early spring were not yet in leaf, and sunlight filtered through the trees. The quiet was magnificent. Dina walked through the brush and climbed over rocks, going up all the time, until she came to a huge mound of rocks and a clearing. Down below her she could see the village, and beyond the blue water of Long Island Sound.

Her solitude was both sad and wonderful. Never had she felt so alone. Stan wasn't truly with her in this fight, since he was resisting because of his playing, and she sensed that he thought her a little silly. Perhaps she was silly. . . . But was she the one out of step or were they?

Dina sat for a long time, thinking about Stan and herself, about her friends and her parents and their friends. Everything seemed out of focus, nothing was the way she thought it should be. Life was chaotic, and there was nothing that she could hold on to, no one she could trust completely, no one truly to count on.

Finally she drove home, grateful for one thing, her precious car. Without it there would be no getting away; she would be utterly stranded. "Car-crazy girl," Helen called her, and she was right. At home she found her mother writing letters with the inevitable glass of sherry by her side.

"Is it a holiday today?" Mrs. Stacey looked mildly surprised. "Why are you wearing blue jeans? They are so unfeminine and unattractive. . . ."

Dina wondered for a minute if explaining the situation to her mother was worthwhile. Of course, sooner or later she'd have to know, in spite of her vagueness.

"I'm suspended from school," Dina announced bluntly. "For wearing blue jeans. We're supposed to wear skirts." If she had expected a logical reaction from her mother, she knew despondently that she only had been kidding herself.

"But you always wear skirts, my dear. I don't understand." The word suspended had gone right by her befuddled brain.

Patiently, Dina explained to her mother the school ruling about attire, and that, because she thought it was unfair, she had deliberately broken it. Mrs. Stacey seemed to be trying to concentrate, but Dina knew her mind was wandering. In the middle of what Dina was saying her mother picked up a letter on her desk and said, "I had a lovely letter from your grandmother. You must write to her."

"You're not paying attention to what I'm saying." Dina's patience was running out.

"But I am, dear. It all seems so silly. You've always worn skirts, so you'll go right on wearing skirts, and there's nothing to worry about. Since you're home today I wish you'd clean out your closet, and if you need any things shortened I'll give them to Mrs. Adams. She's coming this afternoon to pick up some clothes of mine."

"Mother, don't you care that I've been suspended from school?" Dina demanded bluntly.

"It won't hurt you to be home for one day. There's a lot you can do around here." Mrs. Stacey sipped her sherry thoughtfully. "After you do your closet, you can write to your grandmother, and there are a few errands you can do for me in the village. I don't feel quite up to going out today. Stop fiddling with your hair. You can give it a good brushing too."

Dina turned away with impatience and frustration. There was no use in trying to discuss anything serious with her mother. Upstairs in her room, she sat down at her desk and tried to think things out. Her mind kept wandering to what was going on at school, what Helen and her friends were doing, and what she was missing. The most important thing, she decided, was to study for her college board exams next Saturday. But concentrating was almost impossible. Her mind also kept going back to the woman downstairs, her mother. Where had she missed the boat with her own life?

As far as Dina knew her mother had married a man of her choice, man she had been in love with; he had been successful in the business world, and she had two presentable children. Why did she sit in her house and drink sherry all day, dreaming presumably of her girlhood beaux? Dina became frightened when she thought about her mother. Mrs. Stacey had a good mind, she had gone to college, she used to read books and to go out to the theater. Why had she allowed her life to grow so empty? Would Dina end up this way too, an unhappy woman, wasting all her days in a befogged world of sherry and trivialities?

Everything within her cried out no; she longed for

action. Her mother's inertia was what made her want to fight life at every turn. It made her want to rush in head on and demand that something be done, that a conclusion be reached. She had no patience for waiting, for measuring each step, for vague results.

Not able to bear the silence of her own thoughts any longer, she went to the phone and called Stan. He was discouraging. "My mother called up my stepfather right away, of course," Stan told her, "and he kept me on the phone for an hour giving me the works. He's going to throw me out of the house if I don't cut my hair," Stan said morosely.

"Oh, Stan!" Dina was excited, but shocked. "He can't do that!"

"Why can't he? He says I can get a job and support myself. I can too."

"I'll bet you can. You can get a playing job in a minute."

"I'm not so sure." Always against her recklessness he became cautious. "Anyway I don't know if I want to spend my life playing a guitar. I always wanted to go to college. I'm not about to throw that away so fast."

"You can go to college if you want to. You could make some money playing, and then go to college."

"Yeah, yeah. In about a hundred years I'd have enough money to go to college."

"But you're not going to cut your hair, are you?" Dina's voice was entreating.

"I haven't yet. But I don't know. I'm not going to box myself in for a stupid reason."

"It's not stupid." Dina was indignant. "You're defeated before you start."

"But there's nothing to win, you idiot. Mann's not going to change the rules for us. So we'll be out. He doesn't care if we never come back to school. And the parents won't fight. . . ."

"Then why didn't you cut your hair right away?" Dina demanded.

"I guess I was making a gesture. I couldn't take the regulation without doing anything."

"An empty gesture," Dina said with irony. "Well, I'm not giving up so easily."

As soon as she hung up the phone after talking with Stan, she called up Harry. "Stan's giving up."

"He's on the verge, I know. So are Mike and Bob."

"What are we going to do?"

"I don't know. My folks are mad, but they won't object alone."

"Come over and let's talk about it," Dina suggested.

"Okay," Harry agreed.

A few minutes later Harry was sitting in Dina's room.

She knew when she asked him over that Stan was the subject she really wanted to talk about. "What's the matter with Stan? Why won't he fight it out?" Dina had a worried expression on her face.

"He's too smart," Harry said loyally. "Stan is stubborn, but he's not going to let himself be pushed into a corner. He says he'll louse up the exams so he won't get into college, and wearing his hair long isn't worth it. He's got a point, you've got to admit." Harry, who could not sit still, was walking around the room while Dina sat cross-legged on her bed.

"Well, he's a big disappointment to me," Dina said disconsolately.

"You've got to take Stan the way he is. You can't change him," Harry advised.

"Why not? People do change, and a girl can be an influence on a boy, don't you think?"

"In some ways," Harry conceded. "But a boy can also influence a girl."

"Stan does, but he gets me mad," Dina said, her eyes perplexed. "He never gets excited. I get all worked up about things, and he stays so calm that he drives me crazy."

"That's the way he is, and that's the way you are. You ought to make a good team."

"You and I are more alike," Dina said. "You get excited too."

"We'd drive each other wild if we ever went together." The idea amused them both. Dina liked Harry very much. He was warm and lovable and full of bounce. She felt at ease with him, because he didn't tie her up emotionally the way Stan did.

That evening, when Mr. Stacey came home, his attitude was quite different from her mother's. He was very angry with her for what she had done. "It's that boy Stan's influence," Mr. Stacey said, pouring himself a highball. "He's no good. Tom Hennessey is having his hands full. All that boy cares about is playing his guitar. You'd better get yourself some new friends. Your mother would like to give you some nice parties, but not if that long-haired, rough crew you hang out with is going to be invited."

"You are too ridiculous." Dina was in a rage. "Stan and the group are the best boys in town. The only thing you and Mr. Hennessey have against them is the way they wear their hair and how they dress. Well, that's the style now whether you like it or not, and Mr. Hennessey doesn't seem to object to Stan's making money from his playing. I don't want any of mother's parties. I know her kind of party, the kind she had when she was a girl. . . . She thinks we're still babies, and the boys and girls are going to play charades or something. No, thank you."

"Don't be so disrespectful," Mr. Stacey said, his red

face almost bursting with indignation. "You go back to school tomorrow morning dressed the way you should be."

"And what if I don't?" Dina asked.

"There is no such possibility," her father said emphatically. "That's enough now, Dina. I'm pretty tired when I come home from work, and I'd like to relax." He sat down with his drink and picked up the newspaper.

Dina flounced out of the room with tears of anger blinding her eyes. It was almost time for dinner, but deliberately she went outside and got into her car. Her parents made no sense to her, no sense at all. She stepped on the gas and drove the car recklessly out of the driveway, barely missing one of the posts at the entrance.

Dina speeded through the winding roads until she came to the highway, wondering if anyone would care if she got killed. Maybe an accident would shake up Stan, and her parents, too. Maybe then her mother and father would sit up and take notice, forget about what she wore or how her boyfriend cut his hair. Maybe it would make them really care about her and all the teeming emotions constantly churning inside of her. But then their understanding would be too late. Tears came into her eyes as she thought of them standing at her grave, yearning to bring her back to life and crying with tragic remorse and regret at how little they had cared for her or known her while she was still alive.

Her mournful thoughts were interrupted by the sound of a familiar siren behind her. The officer in the police car motioned her to pull over to the side of the road. "Let me see your license. Your registration?" She'd heard the routine before.

"The speed limit here is forty-five miles an hour. Can't you read the signs? You were going over sixty-five." This time her tears and her wiles were of no avail. The officer unsmilingly made out a ticket for her. "This will mean automatic suspension of your license," he said grimly. "It'll be up to the judge to decide for how long." He handed her the piece of white paper. "You'll have to come to this town at eleven o'clock in the morning the day after tomorrow with a parent or guardian. You understand?"

Dina nodded her head. "Isn't there something I can say to persuade you to give me another chance?"

"Sorry miss, but in this state it's the law. Speeding means that your license automatically is taken away, especially in the case of a teen-ager."

The last word upset Dina more than anything else. Teen-agers, teen-agers! The whole world seemed to be against them. I suppose if someone older were speeding, he'd get away with it, she thought angrily. The police are unfair.

The ticket was the last straw of an unhappy day. Dina felt defeated and crushed. Worried about reporting the ticket to her father, she was in a foul mood when she came home and found Stan waiting for her. She stared at him with some contempt. "So, you've cut your hair. I suppose you all did."

"All except Harry. But he'll come along."

"You're so sure of yourself, aren't you? You think everything you do is right, and you can make other people do what you want. Well, you can count me out. I don't turn about face the way you do."

"Now, wait a minute," Stan said calmly. He looked different with his hair shorter. It had not been trimmed in a crew cut, and he still had plenty of hair; what bothered Dina the most was that he looked more attractive than ever. The lines of his long face were stronger and more masculine. "Just wait a minute before you get excited. I'm perfectly willing to admit that we've taken a defeat. But we have to weigh the pluses and minuses. They've got us in a squeeze. First of all, there aren't enough of us. If a whole bunch of kids had refused to go along with the rules, or if more parents were willing to back us up, maybe we'd stand a chance. But this way we'd be jerks to screw up our college boards."

"How do you know you wouldn't win?"

"What can we win? Nobody's going to change the rules for us. Don't be an idiot."

"But sometimes you have to fight even if you're a small

minority. Even if you're going to lose. The fight itself can be important."

"You're talking in generalities." Stan was perched on the porch rail, the wind blowing his hair across his forehead, his blue turtleneck sweater barely visible in the twilight dusk. "Some fights are worth losing and some are not. There are no hard-and-fast rules."

"I admire Harry. He's got more guts than you have."

"Thank you. Thank you very much."

The two stared at each other for a full minute or two. "Sorry you feel that way about it," Stan said stiffly.

"How do you expect me to feel?" Dina's voice was cold. "Do you expect me to say hurrah and clap my hands, because my boyfriend, who is the first to criticize others for being conforming sheep, makes a gesture against stupidity, and then backs down the minute someone says boo."

"Nothing anyone said made me change my mind," Stan answered. "I thought out the consequences myself and decided that holding out didn't make sense. Not worth it."

"Then I guess you and I have very different ideas about worth," Dina said.

"So we have different ideas. We've had them before. That's nothing to get excited about."

"My ideas may not be important to you, but they are to me." His complete calmness was getting her angrier and angrier. "I am excited, and I'm glad. I'm glad I'm not an empty sack like you. I like people who get excited. That's why I like Harry. He carries excitement with him. You act as if there were something wrong about getting excited. You walk around so removed and aloof you give me a swift pain."

"I'm sorry if I give you a pain." Stan jumped down from the railing and stood facing her. "I think this whole conversation is ridiculous. Do you want to go to the movies with me tonight?" Their eyes met. Dina took hers away first.

"I don't think I want to go to the movies with you to-night—or any other night." Dina spoke slowly, deliberately.

There was a long silence. "Do you mean that?" Stan's voice was equally deliberate.

"Unlike some other people," Dina said, "I'm in the habit of saying what I mean." Her heart beating rapidly she turned and walked into the house, thinking of what she had done with a sense of horror. If she had spoken that way to any other boy, he'd come running in after her. But not Stan. He wouldn't give in. From inside the house she watched him jump down the porch steps lightly and get into his car and drive away. There was no sign, no sign at all, to betray his feelings.

Up in her room, after dinner, Dina stared out the window. Her own car was still standing in the driveway looking so gay and ready for fun that she wanted to weep. There would be no more fun. Her car would be forbidden to her, she had taken an insane, irrevocable step with Stan, and she was left with the ignominy of having to retract her position at school. Her spirits fell to the bottom. Life could not sink to any lower depth than at this moment.

She wished she had Barney, her horse. Her mother had been right; since the car had arrived she had stopped riding him. As a result, her father had put him in a stable to be sold. Galloping through the woods with him would have been a comfort, but he was gone. There was nothing and no one to turn to. Jed had been right too. She had completely outgrown her stuffed animals; they were merely sentimental objects that decorated her room.

What had possessed her to be so final with Stan? She knew already that the argument had been due to his catching her at the wrong moment, but she couldn't figure out how to retreat from her decision. He would stand firm and not get in touch with her, and she was too stubborn and proud to go to him.

"You're a dope," Helen said to her on the phone, giving her small comfort. "Why don't you tell Stan right now that you didn't mean what you said? The longer you wait the harder it'll be."

"But I can't. I can't call him now. I could kill that Mr.

Mann. Everything is his fault. I do think Stan is giving up too easily and quickly, so I can't tell him I'm sorry I said he was gutless."

"But you didn't have to break off with him," logical Helen told her.

"I know I didn't. I guess I'll just have to suffer," Dina said morosely.

"You've always said you wanted to experience everything, even being unhappy. Now's your chance." Helen's voice sounded quite cheerful.

"I didn't expect the opportunity to come so soon. And everything at once."

Dina still had to face telling her parents about getting the ticket for speeding.

5

Her parents' reaction to the ticket was milder than she had expected when she spoke to them later that evening. This fact caused another disturbance: they never behaved the way normal parents should.

"I'll call up Tom Hennessey and see what he can do," her father said.

"What do you mean? What can he do?" Dina asked.

"I don't know. I'll find out." Mr. Stacey spoke with some irritation.

"I mean what do you think he can do? Fix it?" Dina asked suspiciously.

"I said I don't know. I'll talk to him right away."

Her questions were more annoying than the ticket, but Dina persisted. "I don't want him to do anything for me. I don't like him."

"I don't care whether you like him or not," Mr. Stacey said angrily. "You're in no position to be choosey."

"I can be as choosey as I want," Dina said indignantly. Her father glared at her and finally she shut up.

Dina fidgeted while her father phoned Mr. Hennessey. Their conversation was brief. "He can't do a thing," Mr. Stacey reported. "They've very strict about speeding tickets, especially those given to minors. You'll have to drive her and appear in court with her," he said to his wife.

Mrs. Stacey looked alarmed. "What good will I do?"

"She can't drive herself; her license will be suspended. And she has to have a parent or guardian appear with her."

"Oh dear, I do hate that long a drive. Dina, why did you get a ticket? It's so inconvenient. . . ." Her mother's voice trailed off.

Dina turned away in disgust. She had expected a lecture about reckless driving and speeding, but that aspect had been glossed over. The *inconvenience* was what bothered them!

She jumped to the ringing of the telephone. Maybe it

was Stan, maybe she was all wrong, maybe he was calling up to tell her to forget what she'd said. . . .

It wasn't Stan; it was Harry. "What are you doing?"

"Nothing."

"Can I come over?"

Dina was relieved not to have to spend the evening sitting with her parents. When Harry arrived, the first thing she noticed about him was that he had not cut his hair.

"I see you're fighting it out," Dina said happily.

"I don't know for how long. My mother's going to see Mann tomorrow. We'll see. Stan said you broke off with him." His bright, lively eyes were fastened on her face.

"He didn't waste much time spreading the news," she said gloomily. Hearing the words from Harry made it seem too final and real. Against her better judgment she had been waiting, waiting for the phone to ring, for Stan to call. But now knowing that Stan had already told Harry, she had to give up hoping. Stan's pride would never permit him to call.

"He's pretty upset. He had to tell someone." Harry was walking around the room, picking up objects and putting them down.

"Is he really very upset?" Dina's hopes soared for a moment.

"You know Stan. He pretends to be calm, but he isn't. Why'd you do it?"

"He got me mad, because he gave up about his hair. He's not fighting at all."

"I know. But don't think he hasn't got the guts to put up a fight. Stan's a cool cat; he's not going to let anyone get him into an uproar over nothing. He reasoned out the situation and he made his decision, and there's no changing him."

"But you don't agree with him, do you?"

"As a matter of fact, I don't. But that doesn't make him wrong and me right."

"You're a good friend to Stan," Dina said with some envy. She didn't believe she had any such friend, not even Helen. Helen, she suspected, would be critical of her and would not stand by her. She wondered if boys were more loyal than girls, and she decided they probably were. A sudden thought came to her. "Did Stan ask you to come here?" She didn't hide the eagerness in her voice.

"No, he did not." Harry's mobile face was serious. "Seeing you was strictly my own idea."

"Did you have something particular in mind?" Dina's eyes met his.

He shook his head. "Not really. I guess I had some thought that maybe I could help patch things up."

"I'm afraid Stan's going to have to do that himself. If he was that ready to accept something I said in a bad moment —and he knew I was in a foul mood—then he must be pretty anxious to break up himself. Otherwise, he wouldn't have accepted it so quickly."

Harry laughed. "Come on, Dina. Stop talking yourself into something. You did it, and you'll have to undo it. But I'm keeping out of the argument."

"It probably won't hurt me to date some other boys for a change," Dina said, wondering to herself if anyone would ask her out.

"Like who?" Harry had a teasing, mocking look on his face.

"Like anyone who asks me."

"How about me?"

Dina's turn to laugh had come. "That's an interesting idea. Wouldn't it be kind of awkward?"

"Why?" Harry was pretending innocence.

"You're such a good friend of Stan's."

"I'd be keeping you on ice for him. At least, you wouldn't be going out with someone else."

"I wouldn't guarantee that. Besides, what makes you think Stan wants me kept on ice? He thinks we're finished, doesn't he?"

"You two will get back together again." Harry spoke casually, but his words gave Dina some comfort. "Come on," Harry said, "let's go out someplace now. I'm sick of this room." Harry couldn't stay in one place for long.

They drove in Harry's car to a little place on the highway with a jukebox. Harry danced the way he did every-thing else, with tremendous energy, and while he was a little shorter than Dina, they made a good team. No one could stay down in the dumps for long with Harry. Much to her surprise, Dina found that she was enjoying herself in spite of her sadness over Stan. She could never feel about Harry the way she did about Stan; Harry was too much like her, too much on the surface. He held nothing back and let his emotions run away with him—she loved Stan's quiet introspection, his moods, and his depth—but she was grateful for Harry's attention and friendship.

They danced furiously until they wore themselves out. Afterward they talked incessantly and laughed a lot. Dina knew that part of her pleasure in the evening came from associating Harry so closely with Stan.

"What about tomorrow? You going to school?" Harry asked in a serious moment.

"I don't know. If you stay home, I'll stay home," Dina said.

"I'm staying home. My mother's going to see Mr. Mann."

"My mother will have a fit if I stay home again, but I will anyway. What are you doing about the college boards?"

"Let's study together. Come over to my house," Harry suggested. Dina agreed.

"And the day after tomorrow I have to go to court with my mother." Dina told him about the ticket.

The next day Dina and Harry waited anxiously at his house for Harry's mother to return from school. "I'm a melancholy optimist," Dina said. "I don't truly expect anything good to happen, but I keep hoping it will."

Mrs. Osborne had no good news when she came home. "He won't budge an inch," she told them. "I'm afraid you kids will have to give up. I told him you'd be back in school tomorrow, Harry." Harry took after his mother. She was just like him: squarely built, warm and outgoing, and bursting with energy. "You'd better go downtown and get a haircut."

Harry's bright face was gloomy. "It's a dirty deal when a fella can't even wear his hair the way he wants to anymore. Talk about regimentation. Here it is. The teachers better not talk about totalitarian states to me. If the principal can tell me how to dress and how to cut my hair, he'll be telling me how to think next."

His mother laughed. "Every society teaches its young how to think according to its own culture. Indian tribes taught their children their own ways, and the so-called totalitarian states do the same. We're no different from either."

"I thought we were supposed to think for ourselves, independently," Dina said.

"Only up to a certain point," Harry said mockingly.

"We're supposed to think for ourselves so long as they like what we think."

"Who's *they*?" Dina demanded.

"The powers that be," Harry told her. "Sometimes they are your parents, sometimes the school, sometimes the party in government. We kid ourselves if we think we're truly a free society. There's no such thing."

"I'm free," Dina insisted. "No one's going to tell me what to wear."

"Don't be ridiculous. Your mother's been telling you right along. And now Mann is. You've got to come back to school, or you'll never get into college. The situation is that simple. They've got us licked."

Dina didn't answer. She knew Harry was right, but he didn't make her feel any better about what had happened. The whole world seemed upside down to her: parents whom she was supposed to obey and respect, drinking their way through life; a society that was supposed to be free, regimenting young people. Even she was mixed up, feeling one way about Stan and acting the opposite. Everything was all cockeyed. Nothing was right.

Much as Dina dreaded going to court with her mother, she was relieved not to have to go to school the following morning. Giving up was not easy for Dina. If she'd had her way, the entire school would have gone on strike and not attended classes until the rules were cancelled. She couldn't understand the general sheeplike acceptance. Why hadn't Stan been a fiery leader and got everyone to stand up together and fight? But Stan was Stan, and she had only to close her eyes to see his steadfast gaze, his calm assurance that he was making a wise decision. Why couldn't she stop thinking about Stan!

The ride to the traffic court was long and dreary. Dina hated driving with her mother, who was a slow and nervous driver. Afraid to pass a car, weaving across the white line. . . . She's the one who should have her license taken away, Dina thought, not I. And her mother's inconsequential chatter was boring. It had nothing to do with anything; she was unaware that Dina was tense with worry about what was going to happen.

"Dina, you're not listening to me at all. I was telling you about my coming-out party. I wanted something different, not just a party in a hotel, so we waited until the summer. It was one of those perfect summer evenings. I was so lucky . . ."

"Mother, if you're going to pass that truck, pass him. Don't hang on his tail."

"Don't tell me how to drive. I'm afraid of those big trucks. But as I was saying, we even had a full moon. We never put up the canopy my mother had for dancing outside. I always think she was a little sorry. It was such a pretty canopy, covered with lovely pink roses, but we did use the small one for the orchestra."

"Don't go out now. There's a car coming the other way," Dina shrieked.

"Don't yell at me that way. That's what causes accidents." Mrs. Stacey pulled the car back into line. "Your voice can be very shrill, Dina."

"I'd rather yell than get killed."

"You do exaggerate so. I've been thinking that you should have a graduation party. It would be almost like a coming-out party. I know you don't want that," Mrs. Stacey added hastily, "but we could have a lovely party with tables out on the lawn and a place for dancing. You young people don't know what real parties are like."

"Mm . . . maybe." Dina was wondering if she and Stan might be back together again by graduation. She couldn't imagine having a party without him. It would be dead, dead, dead.

"You youngsters are so blasé. We adored parties when I was your age." Mrs. Stacey's pale face frowned in irritation.

"I am not blasé. Anything but. We get excited about different things, that's all."

"Ugh. You get excited about cars and politics and things like that. You don't have fun. . . . Oh, the fun and the parties we used to have. We had country club dances every weekend, and I always had so many partners."

"We like to stick to our dates, and we don't enjoy big dances." Dina felt unexpected sympathy for the anxious woman beside her. The small gleam that lighted up her mother's eyes when she talked about her own youth was touching and sad. Dina regretted the emptiness of her mother's life, and the thought suddenly occurred to her that her mother wanted the party for herself as much as for Dina. And why not? Dina thought. If it will make her happy, give her something to think about. . . . There was little enough that she did to give her mother pleasure. Whose fault it was that they couldn't communicate with each other no longer mattered, but a small thing like a party could be a bridge that might bring them closer together.

"A graduation party would be very nice," Dina said aloud.

"Would you really like it?" Mrs. Stacey's eagerness was expressed in her voice and on her face.

"Sure, if you'd like to give it." Dina felt warmed by a wave of tenderness, as if her mother were the little girl and she the older woman.

The courthouse was an old, white building set behind tall trees on a lovely town green. Dina and her mother had to sit and wait their turn, and Dina grew more nervous by the minute. She saw the stern-faced police officer who had given her the ticket up near the judge's chair. When her turn finally came, she and her mother stepped up to stand in front of the judge. In a meek voice Dina pleaded guilty. She was given a fine of fifty dollars, a brief lecture from the judge, and, as the offense was her first, her license was suspended for only thirty days. The whole procedure took a matter of minutes.

Dina felt lighthearted when they came out of the courthouse into the bright spring morning. "I thought it would be much worse," she said.

"Fifty dollars is a lot of money," her mother remarked.

Probably less than they spend on liquor in a week, Dina thought to herself, thinking also that giving up her car for a month was a greater hardship.

On the drive back she and her mother talked about the party. Having something that they could discuss together was nice and Dina found that the ride home was much less boring and passed more quickly.

Only when she got home did she consider having to return to school the next day. Accepting defeat was not going to be easy, and the greatest ordeal would be having to see Stan. The mere thought of meeting him face-to-face made her tense with nervous excitement.

6

"Hello."

"Hi."

Stan and Dina faced each other in study hall. He glanced down at the dress she was wearing, but he made no comment. She thought he looked tired. Tired and terribly attractive, his long face tanned already by the spring sun, his half-closed eyes impersonal. "Sorry about your ticket."

"I suppose Harry told you." They were both self-conscious, embarrassed, neither of them knowing what to say.

"Guess I'd better study," he said, opening a book.

"Lots of luck on Saturday," she said.

"Yeah. Thanks. You too."

After the study period was over, he got up and walked out. Just like that, she thought, with not a word.

"He wanted an excuse to break up," she said to Helen on the bus home. "Otherwise, he'd make some sign. He'd at least want to talk to me."

Helen shook her head. "Not Stan. Once you told him you didn't want to see him, wild horses wouldn't drag anything out of him. He'll never let you know how he feels."

"I can be just as stubborn as he can," Dina said. "Besides, I'm having fun with Harry."

Helen gave her a sidelong glance. "You're not wasting any time, are you?"

"Harry and I are strictly platonic. Really good friends. Seeing him makes me feel in touch with Stan."

As the weeks went by Dina saw a great deal of Harry. He was the one who celebrated with her when she got her driving license back at the end of thirty days. He wanted her to take him to the famous Samoa, but Dina couldn't get herself to go there. It was still sacred ground that belonged to her and Stan.

Who had said what to each other, in her argument with Stan, faded into the past, but the fact remained that something had caused them to drift apart. Perhaps they both needed a respite from the highly charged emotional feelings and tensions between them. . . . Dina and Harry analyzed the situation from every angle, until Harry advised Dina to stop talking and thinking about Stan. "Forget about him for a while," Harry said. "If you get together again, okay, but in the meantime use this time to find out how you really do feel."

"I know you're right," Dina agreed, "but easier said than done."

She always wanted to know if Stan was going out with other girls. "He sees some girls," Harry told her, "but nothing serious." That information alone was enough to throw Dina into a state of depression. She felt that she had carelessly let Stan slip away from her, and her inability to bring him back left her with a desperate sense of frustration. Losing without putting up a fight went against her whole nature, but this instance was one in which she didn't know what move to make.

The boys had a playing engagement in a town about fifty miles away, and Harry suggested that Dina ride out with him on Saturday night. He said that he'd ask Helen and Timmy to come along, so that Dina wouldn't have to sit alone while he played. "But what about Stan?" Dina asked.

"What about him?" Harry shot right back.

"He'll be there, won't he?"

"Of course, he'll be there. So what? He lives in this town. You see him at school. You can't keep ducking him. Come on."

Dina agreed. She went through her closet that Saturday afternoon, putting on dresses and taking them off. Nothing seemed exactly right. She wanted to look lovely for Harry —his friendship kept her buoyed up and saved her from a state of constant depression—but she also wanted to look especially glamorous to Stan. She wished she had something new that Stan hadn't seen before. As she studied herself in a wild print dress she had worn only a few times she had an inspiration that came from a magazine ad. Hastily she whipped through her bureau drawers until she found her black chiffon scarf. She draped it around her head like a hood and decided it looked stunning with the black, blue, and gray print of the dress. In a flash she was cutting and sewing, until her dress had its own black chiffon hood. The finished effect gave her exactly the right air of glamour and mystery she had been seeking.

She knew her costume was a success when Harry picked

her up. "Wow! Dina, queen of all she surveys." His approval heightened her nervous excitement. Helen and Tim's reaction to the way she looked bolstered up her ego, too. Having such good friends whom she could count on in this crisis was wonderful.

She didn't see Stan until he came out to play with the group. The minute he appeared she started talking gaily with Helen and Tim, chattering away until finally she stopped herself and laughed. "What am I being so gay about?" she said with a frank grin. "I'm dying of nervousness, and I'm not fooling a soul, least of all myself. Helen, do you mind if Tim and I dance?"

"Of course not. Go ahead."

On the dance floor, Tim made his usual laconic remarks, which put her more at ease—until she looked up suddenly and met Stan's eyes. She was sure all the blood drained from her face. There was a world of memory in that one brief glance—everything they had been to each other, Samoa, all their beautiful times together. It lasted only a second or two, and then she was whirling away with Tim, feeling like someone lost in a crowd, being pulled away from the person she should be with.

The rest of the evening had a kind of macabre humorous quality to it. Harry danced with her whenever he could, and Mike and Bob cut in. They were all very attentive; their compliments and good-natured teasing made her feel very much the center of the party. Stan spent his time with a pretty little blond girl, who, his friends assured Dina, meant nothing in his life. Yet Dina was aware of his presence every second of the time, and even while she laughed and talked with the others the hurt was there underneath. The emotional intensity made her feel high, charged up, gave her a feeling of wildness; her wit was sharper, her dancing more abandoned. Once on the dance floor she was nearly flung straight into Stan's arms. The moment was a triumphal one, because she was able to laugh lightly and glide back into her partner's arms. Yet at the same time she had a clear vision of weeping over it later, when she was home alone.

At the end of the evening, after they had dropped off Helen and Tim, Harry said, "How about that place Samoa that you and Stan used to talk about? When are you going to take me there?"

The direct, blunt question took Dina aback. "Oh, that place. You keep asking, but it's private between Stan and me."

"I know it," Harry said, "but isn't it high time you got Stan out of your system?" The car was parked just inside Dina's driveway. Dina turned her face away from Harry's questioning eyes.

"I thought you and I were good friends," she murmured.

"We are. That's why I'm saying what I think. You must be a masochist, the way you enjoy torturing yourself. Either forget about Stan or go and make up with him. One or the other, but what you're doing is ridiculous."

"But everything is not so clear-cut," Dina cried out. "I'm not sure I want to go and make up, and yet I can't forget about him. Maybe I am being ridiculous, but I can't help myself."

"I'm going to make you forget about him," Harry said decisively. He pulled her over to him and kissed her squarely on the mouth. His kiss left her cold and a little embarrassed.

"Harry, please. It won't work. You know how I feel about you. I love you, I really do, but not the way I love Stan. Actually I'm even closer to you; we're more alike. But with Stan—I guess I'm more *in* love than plain loving." She took his hand and held it. "Please, Harry, don't be hurt."

"More disappointed than hurt," he said gruffly. "What about that party you and Helen were talking about? You giving a graduation party?" He kept his arm around her, but obviously wanted to change the subject.

"Yes, I am." Slowly she let herself relax against his arm. "My mother wants to give me a party, and I think it will be fun. What do you think?"

"Sure, it would be fun. Would she hire us to play?"

Dina hadn't thought of that idea. "Would Stan come, do you think?"

"Why not? Business is business. Besides, he doesn't hold any grudge against you."

"I don't know whether I'd like having Stan come to play at my party or not. I'd die if he brought a girl along." Dina let out a long sigh.

"He wouldn't bring a girl. When we play at a private party, none of us bring girls."

Dina's face brightened. "Maybe the Beasts would be fun. I'll think about asking the group and see what my parents have to say. Harry, you're sweet. I really like you very much." She looked up into his face.

"Who wants to be sweet! Kiss of death. But I like you too—more than a lot." He bent down and kissed her gently. "Maybe one of these days you'll forget about Stan, and I'll be around when you do."

Dina shrugged. "Who knows? I wish I could forget about him."

When Dina left Harry, she knew she hadn't spoken the truth. She really did not want to forget Stan; thinking about him as much as she did was a kind of self-torture, but she couldn't stop.

Mr. and Mrs. Stacey were completely opposed to having Stan's group play at Dina's party. Mrs. Stacey wouldn't hear of the idea. "We'll have a professional band, not those boys. You'll have good music, don't worry."

"But I want them. We *like* the way they play. That's our kind of music."

"But not that group," Mr. Stacey said. "I couldn't do that to Tom Hennessey. He's a good friend of mine, and I happen to know he's trying to get that boy to give up playing. I can't turn around and give him a job in my house."

"Tom Hennessey is a clump," Dina said. She argued strenuously, although she knew she was fighting a lost cause. "But the group will be included in the party. We're inviting the whole graduation class, aren't we?" she asked anxiously.

"Of course, the whole class is invited," Mrs. Stacey said. "I wouldn't dream of leaving anyone out. Don't worry, Dina, the party will be the best one you ever went to," she added, wanting Dina to share her enthusiasm.

All Dina felt, however, was relief that at least the problem of inviting Stan to the party was solved.

7

The invitations to the party went out three weeks before graduation. The answers came in thick and fast, and of the thirty-eight in the senior class thirty-two accepted. Mr. and Mrs. Stacey also invited several of their own friends. The graduation exercises were to be held on a Thursday evening, and the party was to be held on Friday night. To her mother's delight, Dina was getting very excited about the plans. The party was formal, which meant that the girls would wear long dresses and the boys white jackets and dark trousers or light summer suits. Dina would have to buy her first formal gown.

Dina and Helen went shopping together for their dresses, with an admonition from Mrs. Stacey that if she didn't like what Dina sent home she would return it. The girls drove to the suburban shopping center and systematically went through the three or four shops that carried evening gowns. By the time each of the girls had tried on eight or nine dresses they were exhausted.

"They all begin to look alike," Dina complained.

"There's nothing really exciting here," Helen agreed. "I want something I won't see anyplace else."

Despondently the girls left and bought hamburgers. Neither one of them knew what she wanted except that it must be something very special. Glamorous.

Then Helen had a bright idea. She remembered an ad she'd seen in a local newspaper. Two young artists were opening a new boutique in a barn, and they designed the clothes, one of a kind, for the young and gay in heart. "That's us," Dina said. "Do you know how to find it?"

"I'm not sure, but we can ask."

After many stops for directions, the girls drove down a long, winding country road until they came to a huge barn with a sign *Riverbank Gallery*. Small children were playing in the yard and they were greeted by a handsome young woman, whose heavy, golden-streaked hair was piled on top of her head. She wore huge earrings and a chic dress, and she was barelegged and barefoot. The barn walls were decorated with oil paintings, and at one end there was a curtain of beads. A nest of swallows was making a clatter overhead.

Dina and Helen were enchanted immediately. They sat on an antique French sofa while the young woman showed them the clothes. The dresses were interesting and dramatic, made of unusual fabrics, and designed with graceful lines. Delightedly, the girls tried them on, and finally Dina settled for a pale green chiffon, over a yellow slip, which floated from the shoulders in willowy folds. "Now you really look like a queen," Helen said. Her dress was an elegant silver brocade, an upholstery fabric, the young woman said, cut high in front and very low in back.

"And our mothers can't take them back," Dina said on the ride home. All during the shopping expedition Stan had been in her mind. Which one would make him sit up and take notice? She was sure that the dress she bought would hit the mark.

The graduation exercises were something that one had to go through and were boring. From the stage Dina could see her mother and father and Jed, sitting next to Mr. and Mrs. Hennessey. They all looked as bored by Mr. Mann's long-winded, banal speech as she was. Her thoughts drifted to the troubles she and her friends had gone through at school recently. Thinking about them made Dina resent the graduation ceremony all the more. Mr. Mann's words about each of them stepping out as individuals into a great democracy, when they had been told how to dress and how to wear their hair, were a mockery. The hypocrisy of the man!

After the ceremony, punch and cookies were served in the lobby. Dina got up her courage to say to Stan, "Are you coming to my party tomorrow night?"

Stan nodded his head. "Sure. Why not?" His narrow eyes were noncommittal.

Dina was flustered. "No reason. I wanted you to come," she added.

"I'll be there," he said.

When Dina opened her eyes Friday morning, her first thought was, It's a warm, sunny day. But she jumped out of bed to examine the sky. In June one couldn't be sure; the day could start off in sunshine and end up with a storm. But the blue sky was cloudless, and there was no foreboding mugginess in the air. The day would be perfect, and so would the evening.

Since Mrs. Stacey was so enthusiastic about the party, Dina had let her handle all the planning. Hattie had been making little canapés, baking and freezing things, all week. Her mother had rented a huge punch bowl and glasses and long tables to be set up outdoors. Dina and Jed were to hang up Japanese lanterns in the afternoon. The small orchestra her mother had arranged for was to play from the wide veranda, so people could hear the music both inside and outside, Mrs. Stacey explained, and the large living room and adjacent dining room were to be cleared for dancing. With the graduation class and the friends Mr. and Mrs. Stacey had invited, about sixty guests were expected.

When Dina came downstairs to breakfast, her mother was already there, her face flushed with excitement. She was acting girlish and gay in a way that Dina had never seen before. "It's such a glorious day," Mrs. Stacey said. "We couldn't have asked for anything better. I can hardly wait for tonight. It's going to be a beautiful party. I have an appointment at the hairdresser's, but if the flowers arrive will you arrange them dear? I put out all the bowls and vases in the pantry. Pick the prettiest and use them first. The long-stemmed flowers go in the vases, and the short ones in the bowls. I'll place them when I come back."

Then Mrs. Stacey took Dina's hand and looked at her wistfully. Dina didn't know what was coming next. "You will do something with your hair tonight, won't you? If you want to come with me to the hairdresser, I'll be glad to have my girl set your hair for you."

Such intensity. Dina was embarrassed. "Thank you, Mom, but I think not. I don't look good with my hair set. But I'll put it up tonight and look respectable, don't worry." Mrs. Stacey's anxiety about Dina's hair was touching.

The most important thing on Dina's mind was Stan. The coming night was going to be crucial, she was sure. Either there would be a reconciliation, or she would know that their breakup was final. She couldn't put her finger on why she felt so certain, nor did she care about the why or wherefore; the conviction was something that she felt in her bones, and the thought of it kept her in a state of nervous excitement all day.

Late in the afternoon, when everything was ready for the party, Dina had to admit that her mother had done a beautiful job. The outside of the house was festive and gay with the lanterns, the pretty tables, and the flowers; inside, the tabletops and silver were gleaming. Dina felt a wave of tenderness as she watched her mother's shining face survey the effect. What a pity they were still strangers, and she continued to be a disappointment. If only her mother had been able to step out of her own generation and understand Dina's!

When Dina put on the long, flowing Grecian chiffon

dress, and piled her hair on top of her head, she hardly recognized herself. She had never worn a dress like this one before. She was used to action clothes, and the evening dress was romantic, theatrical. Feeling as if she were in a strange costume, she couldn't quite decide whether she liked it or not. My mother would like me to look this way, she thought. I don't quite know myself in it.

"Well, it's too late now," she told the reflection in the mirror, grudgingly, admiring the tall, slim, elegant girl she was looking at. Maybe it's a new me, she thought, wondering what Stan would think of her.

But Harry, not Stan, came early and reassured her. "Ka-wow, and everything else that goes with it," he said, letting out a low whistle. "You scare me you look so beautiful," he said earnestly.

"Why do you say that?"

"I don't know. Like you have a sign on, *Don't Touch*."

"I won't fall apart," she said with a laugh.

"Maybe you won't, but I will," he answered with a grin.

"Is Stan coming?" Dina asked him.

"I told you he was," Harry said glumly.

"Don't look so sad."

"I wish you'd forget about Stan."

"Tonight's the night," she said, and then wished she hadn't spoken.

"What's going to happen tonight?"

"I don't know, but something crucial. Forget it. I'm just talking through my hat," she added hastily, not wanting to put a hex on herself. She didn't want to spoil her hopes by talking about them.

Soon after Harry came the others began arriving. The orchestra was playing, the party was in full swing, but still no sign of Stan. Dina danced with Harry, she danced with her father and with Jed, and with Harry again, but always her eyes were fastened on the door, watching. The older people had arrived, and the hired bartender was busy. Her parents had told the young people that the fruit punch was for them, but many were drifting over to the bar, adding something more potent to their glasses. Dina really didn't like hard liquor very much, but in the punch she couldn't taste it, and a glass or two made her feel good.

"He's not coming," Dina said to Harry, dancing with him.

"He said he was. He'll show up. Maybe he's scared of the reception he'll get." Harry glanced over at Mr. Hennessey, who was standing with a group of parents at the bar.

"That's silly. He has nothing to worry about." They were in the dining room, and through the archway Dina saw her father walk across the living room rapidly to the outside door. She wondered why he was in such a hurry.

In a few minutes, when the music stopped, she led Harry back into the living room. What she saw made her heart drop with anxiety, and she clutched Harry nervously. Her father was at the door, his face redder than ever, obviously engaged in an argument with Stan and Mike and Bob. The three boys were just outside the door, their musical instruments in their hands, and Dina knew immediately that Stan was furious. She could see the anger in his face and his blazing eyes. Dropping Harry's arm, she ran across the room, but she was too late. The door had slammed and her father stood in front of it, blocking her from going out.

"What happened?" Dina demanded.

"Nothing to get excited about," her father said, obviously agitated. "I told those boys they couldn't come in here with those guitars. They said they never went anywhere without them, and I said this was one place where they weren't going to go with them. Fresh kids. I can see what Tom Hennessey is up against. I'm going to have to explain to him that I wouldn't let the boy in, but I'm sure he'll agree I did the right thing. We're not going to have them play those things here. We paid good money for a good orchestra. If they want to leave those things in the car, they're welcome."

"Let me out," Dina said. She was trying to reach the door.

Her father looked at her suspiciously. "Don't you tell them anything different, Dina. You hear me? I'm not going to go against Tom and have that boy come here and play. . . ."

Dina was out the door, with Harry behind her, just in time to see Stan's car tearing away from the driveway. She ran forward in her high heels and flowing gown down to the road, where she could see the car vanish around the curve.

Dina sat down on a whitewashed rock that marked the entrance to the driveway. The Japanese lanterns, the pretty long tables, the girls in their bright dresses, the boys in their white jackets were all a blur through her tears. Everything looked unreal, like a stage set or a carnival.

"I hate them," she said aloud to Harry. "I was feeling sorry for my mother today, but they don't care. They're living in their own world; they don't give a hang about us. They don't even try to understand how we feel about anything. My father hasn't the slightest conception of how he just ruined everything for me. I'm a shadow in his life, a shadow that has to be fed and clothed, but that's all. . . ." Emotion was choking her voice. "Harry, I had counted so on tonight!" She broke down into hard, convulsive sobs.

"Dina, please. . . . Dina, don't take it so hard. You and Stan aren't necessarily washed up for good. Your father had the argument, not you."

"No, it was tonight or never. I told you so before. Tonight would have been my chance; it was the right moment. And now it's gone. I'm not crying just about Stan," she sobbed, "but about them too. The stupidity, the hypocrisy. . . . How dare he not let my friends in, because they're carrying guitars? Isn't the party supposed to be mine, isn't the house mine too? I'm not a person to them. They just wanted an excuse for another drinking party for themselves. They could have had it without us, without all this fuss!"

Harry tried to put his arm around her, but she cried all the harder when he touched her. "I'm sorry, Harry. I'm sorry to be spoiling the evening for you."

"Forget it. I wish you'd stop crying. That's not going to do any good."

"I know; I'll stop. . . ." She tried to control herself. "Let's go have a drink. Let's get drunk. I bet my folks are potted by now, and I may as well be too." She stood up and took Harry's arm. Her tear-stained face was streaked with mascara.

"I'm game."

"I feel so miserable. I'd been looking forward so much to tonight. Why doesn't anything good ever happen? Look at them!" Dina gestured toward some of the older couples dancing wildly in imitation of the teen-agers, the men with their ties off and the women with skirts above their knees, exposing veined, bare legs. "Aren't they disgusting?"

108

They went over to the bar, and Harry got them each a highball. "Let's go someplace and sit down," Dina suggested, leading him to a solitary bench in the garden.

"I suppose Stan will never talk to me again," Dina said.

"Forget about Stan, will you?" Harry said gruffly. Dina sipped her drink, but he downed his quickly. "I'm going to get out of this place. This town is stifling."

"But your parents aren't like mine. They're real people."

"My parents are okay. But the whole town is full of phonies. Everyone wants to own a Jaguar and have a swimming pool, but they expect the kids to be earnest and wholesome. Talk about the underprivileged, they've got nothing on most of us in this town."

"Living in a slum or a ghetto's no good either. That doesn't help anybody," Dina said moodily.

"No, of course not. What I'm talking about has nothing to do with rich or poor. Caring is what counts. Tom Hennessey can make a first-class bum out of Stan, but Stan will get all the blame."

"Tom Hennessey and my father. . . . He's no better. I wonder what will happen to Jed. He's going to college, but he doesn't know what he wants to do. I hope he doesn't end up like my father. . . ." Her voice trailed off. Not used to drinking, she felt a little light-headed after her highball.

"I'm going to get another drink," Harry said. "Want one?"

109

"Sure," Dina said recklessly. "Why not?"

She noticed when Harry brought the glasses back that his drink was much stronger than hers. "You're going to get tight," she said, giggling.

"Of course I am. That's the idea. Drown my sorrows."

They sat silently, moodily drinking, and watched the party gradually get more and more disheveled. The pretty tables were stained with spilled punch and littered with used glasses. Cigarette butts dotted the lawn, and the guests themselves were no longer bright and shining. Many of the girls had kicked off their high-heeled slippers and were dancing barefoot outdoors, while the boys had shed their jackets and ties and were in their shirtsleeves.

"Dina, Dina. . . ." She heard her mother's voice calling.

"I'm here, Mother. Sitting here with Harry." She wasn't sure she was up to moving quickly.

Mrs. Stacey came walking toward them. She looked grotesque with her lacquered hair still in place, weaving unsteadily on her high heels, and a vacant expression in her pale eyes. "Dina, your guests are leaving. You should come and say good-bye."

Dina couldn't help laughing. The absurdity of the situation set her off into uncontrollable giggles. Everyone was staggering, the beautiful, elegant party had turned into a boisterous shambles, and her life had been ruined, but she must be a lady and say to each guest, "Good night, I'm so glad you were able to come."

"I don't believe what's happening. I just don't believe it," she gasped. She stood up feeling more light-headed than ever. "Come on, Harry." Gaily she pulled him up beside her. She could see that he was really drunk. "Come, we have to say goodnight to the guests."

"Sure," he mumbled. "Gotta say good night to the guests."

The party broke up all at once, everyone leaving except a few of Mr. and Mrs. Stacey's friends. But Dina, floating and full of excitement, didn't feel at all like going to bed. She could go out and fly through the air, conquer the world; nothing daunted her. I can get along without Stan she thought. I can get along without anyone. . . . I'll show him. The sun will still shine without him, the moon will still be full, Samoa will still be there without him.

Dina had a bright idea. Once and for all she would get Stan out of her system. She would make a gesture to end all sentimentality. Her mind was reeling with great ideas.

"Come on, Harry," she said. "Let's go to Samoa for a swim. Then I'll drive you home. You shouldn't drive anyway."

"I'm fine. I'm okay. Just a little woozy, that's all. You shouldn't drive. You can't even walk straight."

Dina weaved on her feet. "Never felt better. I feel marvelous. Come on. I'll show you Samoa. We'll go swimming."

"Great idea. Marvelous idea."

Dina went to tell her parents that she was driving Harry home. "He drank quite a bit," she explained.

"Take care, baby. Drive carefully," her father said. "Too many drunks on the road." His words were slurred.

"Are you sure you didn't drink too much to drive?" Jed asked.

"I'm fine. Never better. Could drive to the moon. Could drive all night."

"There's no night left. It's four o'clock in the morning," Jed said.

"Oh, good! I'll stay up and see the sunrise!" She skipped away, not seeing Jed's anxious eyes follow her. "A few highballs," she said to herself, "doesn't mean I can't drive."

She was itching to get into the little red car and fly away. Cool, cool water. Forget about Stan. Break the spell of Samoa and bring an outsider to it. No more privacy between herself and Stan.

"Come on, Harry. Let's go."

8

Feeling the wheel in her hands was marvelous. All powerful; omnipotent. A beautiful word, *omnipotent*. A beautiful night; beautiful Harry sitting next to her; off to beautiful Samoa.

"Easy on the curves. Makes me feel sick." Harry's head was lolling.

"Hang on," Dina said. She didn't want to crawl along; she wanted to drive fast, faster, fastest. . . . Almost missing a curve, she went off the road onto the shoulder, but pulled the car right again. "See, I can drive fine," she bragged gaily. "I'm the best little driver there is. I'm a car-crazy girl, but you're as safe with me as in your own living room. Except there you could slip on a banana peel." She giggled at her joke, but there was no sound from Harry. He was asleep, which annoyed her.

She jerked the car to a sudden stop at Samoa, jamming on the brakes. Harry fell forward and came to with a start. "What are you trying to do, Dina?" he growled sleepily.

"Come on out. We're here, at Samoa."

"Lemme alone. I just want to sleep."

"No." She prodded him and opened the door. "We've got to go swimming. It'll wake you up." She virtually dragged Harry out of the car.

It was cold and damp in the cove. Dina shivered in her long chiffon gown, her feet bare.

"Nothing but a bunch of rocks," Harry said, weaving about groggily. "What's so great about this place? Nothing but rocks and weeds. Not going to get me in that water." And he stumbled back into the car.

Dina put one foot into the water and pulled it back, shivering again with the cold. She stood, hugging herself with her crossed arms. Nothing but a bunch of rocks. Harry's comment made her feel infinitely sad. She'd come here to lose Stan, but her yearning for him welled up until

114

her throat was choked with sobs. Harry was asleep in the car. She was alone. Alone, alone. No one in the world could be more alone. What if she walked out into the water and kept on walking. The thought made her shiver some more. The tide was coming in, and the water rolled up and licked her feet, wetting the bottom of her dress, but she didn't move. She stood there, a tall wraith in the night, luxuriating in her misery, until the tears were rolling down her cheeks.

Why was life so painful? Tonight should have been beautiful. All the weeks of preparation. . . . What should have been a lovely party had turned into nothing, and she was here with all hope gone.

Tears fogged her eyes as she backed the car out of the cove. Instead of clearing her head the air had made her dizzy, and she longed to be home in her bed asleep. Harry's house was in the opposite direction from hers, and the thought of bringing him home to sleep crossed her mind for a minute. But then she would be giving in. She could drive, she could drive as well as anyone. . . .

The narrow road was dark and there were many trees. They leaned out across the road trying to engulf the little red car. She stepped on the gas to get away from the murky darkness and the trees. If she went faster she wouldn't feel so sleepy. Around the next curve, the one with the big tree, then Harry's house would be at the end of the road. Too bad Harry had drunk so much he couldn't drive himself home; she was really doing him a big favor. Maybe she was a little bit tight, but she could drive. . . .

Her fuzzy mind shifted from the road back to Samoa. It had been so lonely there, so desolate and lonely; the tears were welling again. She shook her head defiantly. She'd show them, Dina and her little red car. She'd go tearing around town in it and show Stan that she didn't care. She'd show her mother and father and Jed, too. No one cared about her, except maybe poor old Harry asleep beside her, and she didn't care about them. Faster, faster, she pushed her foot hard down on the gas pedal. She would fly away from them all. . . .

And suddenly the big tree was in front of her. "Harry!" She heard her own stifled scream and the grinding jam of the brakes, screeching tires, and a deafening crash. . . .

Excruciating pain. She couldn't move; something was pinning her down, a hideous, horrible weight against her body. Better to sink back into blackness again, not to fight it, breathing hurt her so, but she had to keep on breathing. And then the blackness again. . . .

When Dina opened her eyes she saw a strip of crisp, white, starched uniform. It was on a person. An unfamiliar face, a young woman's face, beneath some fluffy hair and a white cap, came into view; her hand was holding Dina's wrist.

"What's the matter?" Dina asked, because the woman's face looked worried.

"Nothing's the matter." A big smile. "You're going to be all right. You're going to be fine."

"Of course, I'm fine," Dina said, wondering why the woman was reassuring her. And then she realized how much she hurt. Talking hurt, breathing hurt. Her whole body hurt, but there were some places that hurt more than others. When the nurse—now she could see who the woman was—let go of her wrist, she put up her hand to her face, and realized her head was swathed in bandages.

"If you take that thing off my chest, it'd be easier to breathe," she said.

"It's just some strapping. You've got a few broken ribs and a broken shoulder. And some cuts on your face and head, and a fractured leg. You're lucky to be alive," she added.

Dina's head ached terribly, but she was trying to think, to get her bearings, and to remember. "That tree, that great big tree. . . ." Every word hurt, but she wanted to talk. "That tree suddenly moved out into the middle of the road. I saw it move; I swear I did. It just moved out in front of the car. . . ." And then memory came rushing back. She

117

tried to sit up in bed, but she couldn't. "Where's Harry? What happened to Harry?"

The nurse was fussing with the window, and turned around. "Just lie quietly. You mustn't get yourself excited. Your parents are out in the waiting room. I'll go call them in. Poor things, they've been waiting hours for you to wake up."

"How long have I been asleep?"

"I guess they brought you in around five or six o'clock this morning. It's almost three in the afternoon now. They gave you a lot of sedation to quiet you down."

"What was I doing?" Dina asked curiously.

"Nothing much, moaning and groaning. I'll get your parents."

"And find out about Harry," Dina called after her. "I've got to know how he is."

"My poor baby, my little girl. . . ." Mrs. Stacey's face was white and strained, but Dina could smell the sweet sherry strong on her breath. "My poor darling, how do you feel?"

"I'm all right," Dina said weakly.

"Don't make her talk," Mr. Stacey said. After kissing her bandaged head, he paced around the room. "Jed sends his love. They said only we could see you now. He'll come

over later. You'll be all right. Don't worry about a thing."
He was flustered and nervous.

"Where's Harry? How's Harry?"

Dina saw her mother and father exchange quick glances.

"He was hurt, darling," her mother said.

"Was he hurt bad? Tell me." Dina could feel her heart
pounding uncomfortably. That look crossed their faces
again, her mother staring helplessly at her father.

Mr. Stacey cleared his throat. "Well, he was hurt pretty
bad," her father said, walking over to the window and
staring out.

Again Dina tried to sit up and couldn't. "Tell me," she
said. "You're not telling me the truth." She thought she
was speaking quietly, but her voice sounded shrill.

Ominous silence in the room, except for the soft sound
of her mother clasping and unclasping her hands. "The
doctor said it was better to tell her," Mrs. Stacey spoke
hesitantly.

"Doctors don't know everything," her father said gruffly.

Dina's ears were pounding with a great noise. Huge
waves from the sea breaking against her eardrums. Harry's
dead. Suddenly she saw the words in tall, black headlines
on thousands of newspapers rolling off the press: *Harry's
Dead, Harry's Dead, Harry's Dead.* Then her own voice
said aloud, "Harry's dead. And I killed him."

Her father swung around. "Don't say that. It was an

119

accident. If he'd had his seat belt on he wouldn't have been thrown out of the car. It was nobody's fault. It was an accident."

Dina closed her eyes. If she couldn't walk away from people, she could shut them out by closing her eyes. Funny, she'd never thought of that possibility before. But then she could always walk before. Now she couldn't. Still she didn't want to see their eyes staring at her, their eyes saying one thing, their lips saying another. They knew in their heart of hearts that she had killed Harry.

Harry was dead. He'd been lying there asleep next to her, his round, innocent face like a baby's, and now he was dead. She felt foolishly grateful for the pain that made her own body ache, but it wasn't enough. It should hurt more until she couldn't bear it any longer, until the room was filled with her low moaning. . . .

"I'm going to call the nurse and tell her to give her something." Her father's voice sounded very far away.

"Hurry up," her mother said. "She looks awful. I think she's going to faint."

When Dina woke up again, it was nighttime. The room was dark except for one small light burning. Jed was sitting on a chair by the light with a magazine on his lap, but his eyes were on her. He smiled at her when she opened her eyes. "Hello," he said, coming over to the bed.

"Hello." She felt so tired that she knew she was going to fall asleep again soon. Waking up was only waking up to pain: the terrible weight of her body and the terrible weight of her grief. She was foggy about time and space, but her memory was clear on one thing. "I killed Harry," she said to Jed. "What am I going to do? What should I do?" she asked pitifully.

Jed shook his head. "There's nothing you can do. It was an accident, Dina."

"No, it wasn't." She was breathing heavily. She couldn't cry; the pain was excruciating. "It was my fault; I was drunk. I think I was speeding. . . . I had no business driving. Jed, help me. I don't know what to do."

Two shadows emerged from the darkness. Her father came into the light, with her mother behind him. "Don't say that, Dina." His voice was harsh. "You never drink. You just had punch. Nothing but fruit juice. It was an accident, you hear me. Maybe you were going too fast, but speeding is one thing, drinking another."

"But Harry and I *were* drinking. I remember clearly. . . . We were sitting in the garden. You came over to us, Mother. I thought Harry was too drunk to drive and that I was sober. But I wasn't. I was just as drunk as he was. Oh, why didn't we stay home!"

"Dina," her father said sternly, "I'm telling you that you weren't drunk. I saw you before you left; so did your

121

mother. We wouldn't have let you go if you'd been drinking. You understand?"

"You wouldn't have known the difference," Dina said dispassionately. "Everyone was drunk. Just like every other party."

"Now listen, Dina—"

He was interrupted by Mrs. Stacey, her hand on his arm. "Paul, please, you mustn't get her excited now."

"You stay out of this. This is important. You want her to go to jail? What's she going to gain by saying she was drunk? Besides, you know she doesn't drink."

"But I did that night." Dina's voice was low but firm. She was looking up at Jed beseechingly.

"Don't be a fool," Jed said. "You can't bring Harry back. Don't be a martyr. Having a drink or two doesn't mean you were drunk."

Dina closed her eyes. She wished they'd all go away and leave her alone. Jed too. Everything took a special effort, as if she were swimming underwater. Her father's voice was still talking, and she could hear the words as if they were being transmitted from a great distance, traveling through hundreds of miles of ocean.

"Listen to me carefully, Dina. Just as soon as the doctor says you can talk, a state policeman will be coming in to question you. Remember that you only drank fruit punch. Do you hear me?"

Dina turned away her face and didn't answer. Remember . . . remember. . . . The word kept ticking in her head, and at one point she wanted to laugh, but she couldn't because it hurt so much. Her father was begging her to remember what she wanted so desperately to forget, but never never would as long as she lived. The scenes—herself and Harry talking and drinking: herself and Harry getting into the car; Harry's hand curled under his cheek as he slept; his soft, even breathing; and then the tree looming up in front of her—were all etched into her mind with a fearful branding iron; nothing and no one could ever erase them.

"Well, young lady, how's my girl today?" The doctor's jovial voice was cloying, but his deft hands removing some of the bandages were comforting. "Feeling well enough to see the law today?"

Dina looked at him inquiringly, squirming as he gently pulled plaster off her chin. "Your father's lawyer, Mr. Hennessey, wants to come in to see you, and there's a state policeman who's been on my neck. A good-looking young man. Think you can take them on?"

Dina nodded. "I suppose so. I hate Mr. Hennessey, but I suppose I have to see him."

"You don't have to if you don't want to. But he'll be talking to you sooner or later."

"I may as well get it over with."

The bright June sun was pouring through the hospital window, and for a few minutes Dina closed her eyes and enjoyed the warmth of it on her face. But the thought of Harry persisted. Harry would never feel the sun again. . . . That Harry existed no more was hard to believe. Harry was dead. She would never see his smiling, exuberant face again. The tears she couldn't control came rolling down her cheeks.

"Come on girl, none of that. What's done is done. You have to think about getting yourself well." The doctor went on with what he had to do, not looking at her face.

"But I can't stop thinking about him," Dina sobbed. "Whatever I do I think of him. If I taste something good, or I feel the sun . . . or anything. I just want to lie here until I die."

"Come now, pull yourself together. Accidents happen every day. You're too young to talk about death. You can't help that boy now. Think about getting yourself well; you're doing beautifully. In a day or two you'll be able to have all the visitors you want. You can see some of your young friends. That'll perk you up."

"I'm not so sure." Dina had been thinking a great deal about Harry's parents. Would she ever be able to face them? She had wanted to ask her mother and father about them, how they were and if they hated her, but she had never got up her courage to find out. She had a rather grim curiosity about what had taken place. Had there been a funeral for Harry? What were her friends thinking and saying? But she had not ventured to ask. Hiding behind the wall of the doctor's order forbidding visitors was easier and safer. Now the thought of being exposed to everyone was frightening. She was bored and eager to see Helen and Stan, if he would visit her, but at the same time she felt uneasy about facing them. What must they think of her!

That afternoon her father brought Mr. Hennessey in to see her. They both repeated everything her father had said to her before: she was a lucky girl to have come out of the accident alive, nothing she could do now would bring Harry back to life, there was no sense in making the aftermath more painful and difficult for herself and her parents, she had not been drinking. The last point was the most important.

"You will be charged with negligent homicide for speeding," Mr. Hennessey said. "If we're lucky we'll get away with a fine, and that will be it."

"What does negligent homicide mean?" Dina asked. "Doesn't homicide mean murder?"

"Take it easy, girl," Mr. Hennessey said. "Don't make matters worse. Homicide means the killing of one person by another, but in legal terms it is not necessarily murder.

125

Don't get dramatic. Negligent homicide means an accident. That's all you have to remember; the crash was an accident. You didn't want to kill Harry, did you?"

"Oh, no, of course not. But. . . ." She looked at the two men. Her father appeared as much a stranger as Mr. Hennessey. She knew she could never explain to them in a million years all the conflicting emotions that she was feeling.

"But nothing. You don't want to go to jail, do you?" Mr. Hennessey's small eyes were staring into hers.

"Would they send me to jail?" Dina's voice faltered.

"If you behave foolishly, they very likely would. I couldn't stop them. They call it a state farm, but it's a prison just the same." Then Mr. Hennessey added in a cajoling tone of voice. "But nobody's going to jail if you're sensible."

Jail. . . . Dina hadn't actually thought about the possibility of going to jail. The idea terrified her. She had never been in a prison, but what she had seen on television shows was enough to send her imagination into sinister, dark corners. She pictured herself in a coarse, ugly uniform behind bars, in a cold cell, not seeing any sunshine, not being able to walk in the fresh air, without friends. The food would be bad; she would be surrounded by frightening women from the underworld and bullying matrons. Could such things actually happen to her, Dina Stacey, who had never wanted to hurt anyone in her life? The prospect was overwhelming.

She pulled up the covers to her chin. The decision was too much of a burden for her tired body and brain. She wished that there were someone she could talk to whom she could completely trust. Although she knew that her father and Mr. Hennessey were trying to protect her, there was something about their protection that repelled her too. But on the other hand—jail! That such a thing could possibly happen to her, a "nice" girl from a "nice" family, seemed incomprehensible.

Dina lay in bed listening to her father and Mr. Hennessey talking in low voices. She didn't have the energy to try to follow their conversation. Her father was nervous, taking off his eyeglasses and polishing them every few minutes, his ruddy face anxious and worried. Was he afraid that she might go to jail?

After all, what they said was true: it *was* an accident, nothing she said or did now could change what had happened, could bring Harry back.

Mr. Hennessey leaned over to say something to her.

"No, of course, I don't want to go to jail," she said to him. "No, I don't want to make trouble for everyone. Yes, I am very tired. I'd like to go to sleep."

9

Dina was just finishing her light supper when the state policeman came in. A ghastly supper it was typical of hospitals with its lukewarm creamed chicken and mashed potatoes. Mush.

He was young and good-looking, and his voice was gentle. "Tell me in your own words exactly what happened." His chair was pulled up close to the bed, a pencil and pad were in his hands.

"I don't know where to start. . . ." Dina wondered what

128

she looked like. Sometime during the day a nurse had brushed her hair, but she hadn't seen a mirror since the morning after Doctor Loring had taken off the plaster. There had been dark blue bruises under her eyes and a scab down the side of her cheek. She must look a fright.

"Start at the beginning. You were at a party at your house. Why did you drive the boy home? I understand he had his own car there."

"Harry was tired. He was very tired and sleepy. And I wanted to show him something. I wanted to show him Samoa."

The young man looked startled. "Samoa? Isn't that a long way from here?"

Dina was surprised that she could still smile so easily. "It's just the name we—I gave to a little cove on the water. I guess I felt like driving. Oh, if only I hadn't. . . ."

"Why?"

The question startled and frightened Dina. "The accident might not have happened."

"You mean it happened because you were driving? Was there some reason why you shouldn't have been driving?" He was leaning toward her, watching her intently.

Dina laughed nervously. "No, of course not. I mean if I hadn't taken him home the accident wouldn't have happened, that's all. He might have stayed at our house overnight."

"Do you usually have your boyfriends stay overnight when you have a party?"

"No, but it was very late. I don't have parties often."

"You said Harry was tired and sleepy. Had he been drinking?"

"I don't think so. Maybe he had a couple of beers. I don't know." She looked at him, and then glanced away. She knew what the next question would be, and her heart was beating rapidly.

"You were driving very fast. Your speedometer was stopped at seventy-eight miles an hour. Had you been drinking?" The question came casually, sympathetically, as if there were nothing in the world wrong if the answer was yes. His tone implied that they both knew that everyone drank at parties and that he and she both naturally would.

Dina was immediately conscious of the trap, and she yearned to fall into it. But fear had been drilled into her. You don't want to go to jail, do you? You don't want to cause more pain to everyone, do you? Nothing you do now can bring Harry back. . . .

"No, I don't drink," Dina said evenly. Once the words were out, her heart subsided, and she felt a certain relief. Lying had been quite easy.

"But this party was special, wasn't it? Everyone else

130

was drinking. Sure you didn't join in a toast or two?" His voice was less casual, more insistent now.

"The grown-ups were drinking. There was fruit punch for my friends. Some of the boys might have had a few beers."

There was no sign on his face, but she sensed his disappointment. He had mapped out the accident in his mind before he came to see her, and she realized that he had to rearrange his thinking now. "You should have had a test for alcohol, but you were unconscious, and then the doctor wouldn't let anyone near you. . . ." He was talking to himself rather than to her. Obviously, however, he had made a mistake by not insisting on a test, and somehow his omission put them in the same boat; her lie seemed less of a betrayal. If he hadn't made a mistake, she wouldn't have had to lie; the truth would have been known, and no one could change it. She felt more at ease knowing what had happened. The burden was on him as much as on her.

After that the interview was fairly smooth going. Dina told him how they'd left the party, driven to the cove, how Harry had dozed off. When she got to the part about the tree she broke down for a minute or two. He waited sympathetically until she regained control of herself.

"I don't know what happened. I didn't think I was going so fast. Maybe I dozed off for a few seconds without realizing it. All I know is the tree was in front of me and I jammed on the brakes. That's all I remember."

He took her testimony all down on his pad, his face noncommittal. At the end she asked him about the car. He was the first person she dared raise the question with. She couldn't get herself to ask her parents, and she hadn't seen Jed alone long enough. In her mind she had seen the little red car as a twisted-up heap, like the cars one saw in junk piles; yet she kept on hoping it would be all right.

"It's gone. The car is gone," the officer said. "Crumpled up like a piece of paper. Forget the car."

Then, all of a sudden, she started crying for the loss of the car. "It's nothing," she sobbed. "It's only a car, and it doesn't matter—Harry's the only thing that matters—but it meant something to me, that car. I didn't think it would be *all* gone. I thought it could be fixed. I know you think me a fool, crying about a car, but it was mine, my first, and it was special, very special. . . ."

"That's all right. I understand." The police officer patted her arm gently. "Kids get attached to cars."

"I'm not a kid, but I loved that car." She sobbed even harder.

"Sure, of course you did." He stood up, embarrassed, ready to leave. "Take it easy. You don't want to break some more ribs."

"I'm sorry." She lifted her tearstained face and smiled

good-bye to him. He was a nice guy, and he made mistakes too.

The first visitor who came to see her, as soon as the doctor said she could have friends, was Helen. Dina was sitting up in bed, her leg in its cast stretched out in front of her. The two girls embraced.

"Are you all right?" Helen asked.

"Yes, I guess so." There was a strain between them, and Dina didn't know how to begin to ask all the questions that were on her mind. They talked about everything except the accident and Harry for a little while. Finally Dina couldn't stand the mounting tension. "What's everybody saying? About the accident, I mean?" she asked. Helen's eyes were evasive. "Naturally everyone feels terrible. They say it's lucky you didn't get killed."

"I suppose they're saying I should have been killed instead of Harry," Dina said with a flash of insight.

Helen looked uncomfortable. "If they are, it's only because they think you were drunk and had no business driving." The two girls' eyes met. "I'm not going to ask you if you were drunk," Helen said. "I guess I don't want to know."

Dina was quiet. "I wasn't drunk," she said at last, breaking the silence. "It was an accident."

Helen's face brightened. "I certainly am glad to hear you

say that. Now I can tell off those kids who have been talking about you. I told them they didn't know what they were saying, but of course I wasn't sure. What a relief."

Dina stared gloomily out of the window. "What have they been saying?" she asked listlessly.

"Oh, you know, that you'd been drinking, and that's why you were speeding so. That you went off with Harry because you'd had a fight with Stan. A lot of rubbish."

"I didn't have a fight with Stan. My father sent him away." Dina wished that Helen would go. She couldn't stand her sitting there looking so relieved. The decision is made, Dina thought morosely. Now I'm going to have to lie to everyone. I'll never be able to be honest with anyone again. This aspect of her predicament was one she hadn't thought of before. She had always had a straight relationship with Helen, with Stan, with any of her friends. Now there would always be this lie between them; she would always have to be on guard and hide her shame from everyone but herself.

Dina braced herself for the next question she had to ask. She knew her curiosity was a form of self-torture, but she had to know all the grim facts. "Did you go to Harry's funeral?"

Helen nodded her head. "It was very beautiful and very sad. His parents were marvelous, and the minister was terrific. The whole graduating class was there. The family

134

didn't want any flowers. I think there's some talk of their setting up a scholarship fund in his name. For college. He would have been going to Penn this fall."

"Yes, I know. . . ." Dina couldn't contain herself any longer, and she burst into tears. "I can't stop crying," she sobbed. "All I do is cry. I feel so awful. I wish it *had* been me instead of Harry. He was a terrific boy. I can't believe that he's dead, Helen; I can't believe it. Oh, if only I had that half hour to live over again."

"Dina, darling, don't cry so hard. You'll hurt yourself. There's nothing anyone can do. You mustn't carry on so." Helen had her arms around her. The tears were rolling down Helen's cheeks at the same time.

"You're crying, too," Dina said, and the two girls couldn't help but laugh at themselves trying to comfort each other and instead crying together. "Harry would certainly think we were funny," Dina said. She held on to Helen's hand, feeling more at ease with her now and grateful for her friendship. If only she could tell her everything, but her secret was one that she could share with no one.

"I've got to go," Helen said, drying her tears. "There are a bunch of kids waiting to see you. The nurse won't let more than two come in at once. I insisted that I wanted to see you alone, but I guess I'd better give the others a chance now."

Dina was sorry to see her go and wished that Helen could stay with her and give her moral support while she faced the other visitors.

After supper Dina was exhausted. Having visitors had been pleasant, and everyone had been very nice to her, but all the talk was tiring. Her parents were with her now, and she wished they would leave. Her father kept asking, over and over, what she had told the state police officer.

"Don't worry," Dina said wearily. "I said all the right things. All the proper lies."

"Don't talk that way," Mr. Stacey admonished her. Dina closed her eyes and sighed with relief when they left.

Alone, Dina picked up a book, but she couldn't concentrate. As she held the book in her hands her mind wandered. Had her friends looked at her strangely when they'd come to see her in the afternoon? And why hadn't any of the boys from the combo come? And what about Stan? Did Stan hate her, because she'd killed his best friend?

Dina could hear the noise in the hall of visitors' leaving, which meant it must be close to nine o'clock. Someone would bring her a glass of juice and maybe a pill, and then she'd drift off to sleep. . . .

The door opened, and Stan was standing there. She was so surprised she let out a little cry. His face was white and strained.

"Hello."

"Hello, Dina."

He walked over to the bed and looked down at her. "You're all right? You're going to be all right, aren't you?"

"Sure, I'm all right. How did you get in so late? They usually don't let people in after hours." She was making foolish conversation, but she had to do something to fill the silence.

"I came in earlier and waited for your folks to leave. I didn't think your father would like to see me here." He smiled ruefully.

"Forget about my father," Dina said. "How are Harry's parents? I keep thinking about them."

"They're pretty good. Mrs. Osborne said she wanted to come to see you, but she didn't think she was up to a visit yet. They don't hold anything against you, if that's what you're worried about."

"I don't see how they can help it. I'm all right physically, but Stan, the rest of me is a mess." Having him stand there beside her was a tremendous relief. She wished he would bend down and kiss her, take her in his arms, but he simply stood there, next to the bed, looking down at her. The hall was quieting down. "They're going to throw you out of here soon. The nurse will come in and make you go."

"I'll wait until she does." They kept gazing at each other, not saying a word.

Dina broke the silence. "There's so much to talk about. I haven't been able really to talk to anyone. I don't know what to do."

"What's the matter?" Stan asked.

"I've got to talk to someone. I can trust you, can't I, Stan? I mean you won't repeat to anyone, not a soul, what I tell you. It's terribly serious and important."

His eyes were wary. "You can trust me. But don't talk unless you want to."

"I have to. I'll die if I don't." Quickly she described her predicament. She told him that her father and Mr. Hennessey insisted that she hadn't been drinking and that she finally had agreed and repeated the same thing to the state police officer. "But it's not true. I know it's not true, and I can't forget it for a minute." She looked up at Stan's solemn face beseechingly. "What should I do?"

"You seem to have decided," Stan said quietly.

Was there a hint of coldness in his voice or was she just imagining it? "You think I'm doing something terrible, don't you?"

Stan shrugged. "I don't want to pass judgment. You have to figure out whose side you're on. If you want to line yourself up with your father and my stepfather, that's your business."

"That's a lousy thing to say." Dina was hurt.

"I don't want to hurt you." Stan's voice was gentler. "I

wouldn't want to be in your shoes for anything. Whatever you do doesn't matter too much, certainly not as far as Harry's concerned. I'm the last person to ask anyway. I hate everything my stepfather stands for. I hate his finagling and his thinking that he and his clients can buy their way out of any situation. But you should do whatever is easier for you; it honestly doesn't matter too much."

"It matters to me," Dina said softly. "Stan, come here and sit beside me for a minute."

He sat on the edge of the bed and held her hand. They were sitting that way quietly when the nurse came in and told him he'd have to leave.

10

In September Dina was still dressing with difficulty. The cast was off her leg and her ribs were healed, but her body felt stiff and awkward.

"Wear something subdued," her mother had said.

"And make sure your skirt covers your knees," her father had added.

Dina had been annoyed at their concern over how she would look, as if her appearance mattered, but now, studying the contents of her closet, she chose a dark-blue knit suit. It was certainly subdued enough. Ordinarily she wore green shoes and green earrings with it, but today she put on black shoes and left off the earrings.

This day was the big one, the day she'd been dreading all summer, the day her case was coming up for trial. The summer had been lost: half of it in the hospital, half of it at home, all of it feeling low and depressed. Her life seemed shattered and lying about her in small, broken pieces. Nothing had truly healed, nothing had started up again after the accident had occurred.

Her arrest and arraignment when she came out of the hospital was just another unpleasantness that by now had merged into the summer's gloom. Dina and Mr. Hennessey and her parents had appeared before the judge. He gave her a terse lecture and set bail until the date of her trial came up. She had been quiet and controlled in the courtroom, but home in her room she had cried for a day and a night. Two months before she had been a happy-go-lucky girl, and now she was enmeshed in a shadowy world of death and doctors, of arrests and courtrooms. She felt as if she had moved into a life shrouded in evil, with the guilt of murder haunting her soul.

"You mustn't feel guilty about Harry," Harry's mother had said to her, when Dina finally had summoned the courage to see her. "Your life was saved, and you must not waste it now in self-destructive remorse. Then you would double the tragedy."

Mrs. Osborne had been dry-eyed, and she spoke in a steady voice. "God saved your life, and you must make it more meaningful."

Dina had nodded her head in silence, with her eyes lowered, unable to face the steadfast gaze of the woman whose tragedy she had caused. A wall surrounded Mrs. Osborne, as everyone else, and it kept Dina alone and separate.

Even Stan stood apart. Or especially Stan, she thought. That he was the only one who knew the truth hadn't made his company any easier. Stan had come to see her during the summer, and they had not discussed the accident or her drinking, yet the unspoken subject was between them all the time, never diminishing in its impact. So many times she had thought, or imagined, that Stan was staring at her questioningly and then appraisingly, as if trying to judge what kind of person she was. A few times he had started to say something, and then he broke off, mumbling, "Oh, well, you wouldn't understand. . . ." As if they now moved in different worlds and she had taken sides with those he considered his enemies.

"Dina, are you coming down for breakfast?" Her father's voice was impatient, as it cut into her thoughts.

"I only want coffee," she called back, fussing around her

room. She wanted to delay going down, wishing she could disappear and avoid the whole trip.

"We don't know when we'll get lunch. You'd better eat something," her mother called from her own bedroom.

"I'm not hungry," Dina told her.

Dina heard Mr. Hennessey's car pull into the driveway and Mr. Hennessey come into the house. The thought of the hour's drive to the courtroom with those three made her feel sick to her stomach.

And the ride turned out as she had expected. There were long, ominous silences broken every so often by Mr. Hennessey's saying something to Dina that he had already told her before. "Speak up clearly so the judge can hear you. Tell him what happened in your own words. Speak the truth, that's all."

"I wish I could tell him the real truth," Dina murmured.

"You're not going to start that again. Not now," Mr. Stacey said with nervous irritation. "Cut that out, Dina."

Mr. Hennessey started all over again, with exaggerated patience. "You are telling him the truth. Not what you imagine, but what happened. You had a few glasses of fruit punch, that is all. You were tired and you wanted to get home, so you did drive too fast. Admit that honestly."

Brainwashing, brainwashing, Dina thought, but kept still.

The courthouse looked particularly serene set back on its

lovely tree-lined street, the tall maples beginning to turn. Dina wondered how she could feel so awful amidst such peace and beauty. On this day one should go for a walk in the woods, not stand before a judge and tell how Harry was killed.

Dina remembered the courthouse from the time she'd been there with her mother. Her suspended license seemed like a million years ago. The inside was less imposing than the outside, for the walls and benches were bare, and there were cigarette butts on the floor. The room was half-filled with groups of people scattered here and there. Mr. Hennessey went over to confer with the court clerk while Dina and her parents took seats near the front of the room.

"We'll get started qualifying the jury soon," Mr. Hennessey reported back. He had asked for a jury trial because, as he had said, "Judge McCracken is very tough. I wouldn't want to come up before him alone with this case. He's a crusader against teen-agers driving altogether, and a young kid like Dina with a car of her own and an earlier offense for speeding wouldn't stand a chance with him. We're much better off with a jury. They'll be sympathetic, because she's young and remorseful. Some jurors will be parents, who won't want to see her education interfered with."

That many parents might also disapprove of teen-agers driving, occurred to Dina, but she had found out that Mr. Hennessey's decisions were not to be contradicted.

144

There was a sudden silence in the courtroom, and everyone stood up as Judge McCracken came in and took his place on the bench. He was an imposing man in his long black robe with a crop of thick white hair above a lean, ascetic face. His pale eyes were cold and devoid of any visible humor.

"He gives me the shivers," Dina whispered nervously to her mother. She was more frightened than she had expected to be. Nobody looked friendly; the young state policeman who had come to question her in the hospital gave her a curt, solemn nod when she smiled hello to him.

Mr. Hennessey and the prosecutor started questioning the jury. Dina examined the face of each person intently, looking for a clue as to how he or she would react, but she could come to no conclusions. The spinsterly looking elderly lady turned out to be a grandmother with nine grandchildren; her face was stern, but when she smiled Dina thought she might be sympathetic. The group was nondescript: housewives, working men and women, a few professionals. Two persons were disqualified, because someone in their family had been involved in a serious auto accident. Another woman was disqualified, because she had recently received a ticket for speeding herself.

Finally twelve jurors were chosen, and they took their place. None of them paid any attention to Dina; their eyes were on the judge, who was telling them to listen carefully and objectively to the testimony. He said that they had to decide whether the defendant had been negligent or not.

The first witness called was the young police officer, who had arrived at the scene of the accident before anyone else. The police, called by a neighbor, had sent on the message to him while he was cruising, and he found the car thoroughly smashed. The ambulance came almost simultaneously; the boy was dead and the girl unconscious. The officer testified that the car had swerved into the tree, that the morning was clear and dry, and that the speedometer had been clocked at seventy-eight miles an hour.

Then Mr. Hennessey questioned him. "Isn't it true," Mr. Hennessey asked, "that a few years back the highway department was asked to remove that tree because it was a hazard?"

The officer shook his head. "I don't know anything about that."

Dina had never heard this point mentioned, and she wondered if it were true, or if Mr. Hennessey was simply making it up. She couldn't trust him.

"Isn't it true that the owners of the property persuaded someone in charge to let the tree remain?"

"I don't know," the officer said. "I doubt that they could have if the tree were truly a hazard."

"I didn't ask for your opinion," Mr. Hennessey snapped.

"Was there any mark on the tree, such as a reflector

strip, that would warn motorists?" Mr. Hennessey continued.

The police officer shook his head. "No, sir. The tree does not obstruct the road."

"Objection! Strike that out," Mr. Hennessey growled, "and keep to the question." The judge agreed to having the officer's comment stricken from the record, but Mr. Hennessey was red with anger. "Young twerp," he muttered, when he came back to join Dina and her parents. But even though he had not helped her any, Dina's sympathy was with the clear-eyed young policeman.

The prosecutor cross-examined the neighbor who had heard the crash and called the police and the hospital, and he cross-examined the interne who had been on the ambulance. Finally Dina went to the witness stand. "Just speak up clearly, and don't be nervous," Mr. Hennessey warned her at the last minute.

Dina was terrified as she walked up to the stand. She felt the twelve pairs of eyes of the jurors fastened on her. Solemnly she put up her right hand as instructed and swore to tell the whole truth and nothing but the truth.

The prosecutor was a clean-cut, fairly young man with a sharp nose, a dimpled chin, and deeply set brown eyes under a high forehead. Dina had no strong feeling about him one way or another, finding him neither friendly nor unfriendly. But she sensed a brisk determination in him and a high-powered brain that frightened her. I'm no match for him, she thought to herself.

He started off easily and gave Dina a sympathetic smile. "Please tell us in your own words exactly what happened, Saturday night, June eighth. You were at home, having a graduation party, weren't you? Start with that."

"Yes, we had a graduation party. All of the senior class was invited. . . ." Dina spoke in a low voice. "The party was like any other. . . ."

"Nothing unusual happened at the party? Did anything happen to upset you?"

"No-o. Nothing happened. Nothing at all," she repeated, hoping she wasn't emphasizing the denial too much. "We all had a very good time. It was late when it started breaking up."

"What time would you say?"

"I'm not sure. Perhaps around three or four o'clock. Harry and I were sitting out in the garden when some of the kids left."

"What were you doing in the garden?" His voice was gentle.

"Just sitting and talking. When we came in a lot of people had gone. Harry seemed very tired, and then I got the idea of showing him a little cove I liked and of driving him home. . . ." Her voice sank to almost a whisper.

148

"Speak up louder, please," the judge interrupted.

"Yes, sir."

"If Harry was so tired, what made you want to take him to this cove?" The prosecutor's eyes on her were sharp.

"I don't know. It just seemed like a good idea. He wasn't that tired."

"Did you think he couldn't drive himself home?" The question was thrown at her unexpectedly.

"I—I didn't think about it."

"Weren't you afraid he couldn't drive himself home because he had been drinking? Wasn't he drinking a highball when he was with you in the garden?"

"I don't remember. The kids were drinking fruit punch." One of the women on the jury dropped her pocketbook, and it made a clatter on the floor. Dina looked up quickly, and she sought out the faces of her parents and Mr. Hennessey. The three faces blurred into one, each with the same expression of nervous anxiety. Strained, flabby faces, concentrating, she knew, on only one thing. There was a little movement at the door, and she saw Stan standing there in the back of the room. She caught his eyes, and he smiled at her. Something in his face made her want to cry.

"Weren't some of the young people drinking hard liquor?"

"I don't know."

"Wasn't there a bar and couldn't anyone get a drink?"

"There was a bar, but it was for the grown-ups. I didn't watch who went there for drinks."

"When did you and Harry leave the party?" Dina felt relief that he had changed his line of questioning.

"I'm not sure of the time. I think it was almost four."

"What did you do?"

"I drove in my car to the cove. Harry and I got out for a few minutes. We looked at the water and the rocks. Then we got back in the car, and I started to drive him home."

"Tell me exactly what happened on the way home."

"I just drove. The way I always drive."

"Are you accustomed to driving at seventy-eight miles an hour?" The prosecutor shot the question at her.

"No, of course not."

"Then why, after four o'clock in the morning, when you were very tired from an exhausting party, did you decide to drive along a winding country road at seventy-eight miles an hour? You graduated from high school with a B-plus average didn't you?"

"Yes, sir."

"And you were planning to go to college?"

"A junior college."

"You're a bright, intelligent girl. You had received one ticket for speeding and had your license suspended. At that time you seemed to take your offense seriously and promised you would drive carefully, which apparently you did until that fateful morning. What happened to you that night or morning that caused you to be so reckless as to drive at that suicidal speed and kill a young man with his whole life ahead of him? Why?"

His voice had become sharp and piercing. Dina felt sick to her stomach. I promise to tell the truth, the whole truth, and nothing but the truth. . . .

Whose side do you want to be on, Stan had asked. Whose side did she want to be on? Did she want to line herself up with the pathetic figures of her parents, endlessly running away from themselves into a stupor of alcohol? Did she want to line herself up with blustering Mr. Hennessey, trying to duck every payment that society demanded?

Dina lifted up her face and looked at the prosecutor. She didn't care about him. By tomorrow he would have forgotten this case and be busy with another. She could go on lying to him, and he would never know the difference. In a few months no one would remember any of this testimony. No one except the people who loved Harry. Just those people and herself. They would remember.

The prosecutor's face looked like a fox. He had fox eyes too. The courtroom was very still.

"Speak up, girl, and answer him," the judge said. "We can't wait here all day."

"Yes, I'll answer him," Dina said quietly. "I drove that way because I was drunk. I'd had several highballs that night and I'm not used to drinking. I was drunk." She repeated the words with simple emphasis.

She heard a gasp from her mother. Mr. Hennessey jumped up. "She doesn't know what she's saying. The girl is frightened and intimidated. I ask that the defendant be excused," he said to the judge.

"I am not frightened," Dina said clearly, feeling only the greatest relief she'd had in over two months. "I know what I'm saying, and it's the truth."

There was a stir in the room and the judge called for order and silence. The prosecutor stepped down. "I'm finished," he said with a smile that twisted his mouth out of shape.

"Do you want to question your defendant?" the judge asked Mr. Hennessey.

"No, there's nothing more to say."

Dina stepped down from the witness stand and took her seat. Her mother was crying softly. Her father was flushed with what she could only assume was anger.

"You're a stupid, foolish girl!" Mr. Hennessey said under his breath, glaring at her.

Dina's long lashes covered her eyes. She felt sorry for her mother and father, and her pity carried with it more affection than she had felt for them in some time. Mr. Hen-

152

nessey was simply annoying. Even what she felt for her parents, however, was only peripheral to the central question: what she felt about herself. This decision was probably the most important one I'll ever have to make in my life, Dina thought.

I made my choice, and now I know where I stand. They won't be able to touch me. I don't have to live their kind of life. Mine will be different. I believe I'll know whose side I'm on.

She turned around to see if Stan was still there. He was sitting in the back of the room, and he held up his hand and gave her the sign of victory.

The jury wasn't out long. The foreman came in and announced their verdict of guilty. Mr. Hennessey conferred with the judge, and they agreed on a date, after a presentence investigation, for Dina to come back to court to have her sentence set.

11

Except for the box overflowing with clothes and odds and ends to be discarded, her room already looked as if nobody were living in it. It was obsessively neat: not a pencil out of place in the desk, no papers or books strewn about, no sweaters draped over chairs. The stuffed animals were in a box by themselves, ready to go to the children's ward in the hospital.

154

"You act as if you're never coming back," Helen had said the previous afternoon. "You're only going to be gone ninety days—three months. That's not a very long time."

Dina had smiled. "Three months in prison can seem like a lifetime I imagine. But I'm not complaining. You won't believe me, but when the judge set my sentence I was almost relieved. I didn't think I should get off scot-free. Mr. Hennessey was boiling, but I'm glad he didn't get his way."

"Something happened to you, Dina. You're different."

"Of course, I'm different. You can't go through what I have and remain the same. I'm not sure I *will* come back here, but even if I do, I've cut the cord once and for all."

"You talk as if you hate your parents. Do you?"

Dina's face was thoughtful. "I used to think I did, but I don't. I feel sorry for them. I do hate the way they live. My mother especially." Dina shivered. "She used to scare me; I was afraid I'd end up like her. But now I know I won't. I don't know what I'm going to be or do, but I'm not going to sit around and waste my days."

"It is sad," Helen agreed. "I think you were very courageous to come out in court and say you were drinking. I don't know that I could have. Mr. Hennessey says you would have got off with a suspended sentence."

"I know. But I didn't feel brave, and I'm sure not dying to go to jail. I just did what I felt I had to do, that's all. To feel right with myself."

Dina had no regrets for her statement in court, in spite of the jail sentence. And now, waiting to go off to the state farm for ninety days, she felt calm. A policewoman was coming to pick her up soon, and she wished she'd hurry. She didn't like waiting around; she wanted to leave and get the trip over with.

"Dina. . . ." Her mother was at the door, the inevitable glass of sherry in her hand. "Are you all ready?" Mrs. Stacey's voice was shaky.

"I'm as ready as I ever will be."

Mrs. Stacey came into the room and stood at the window. "I can't believe it," she said with a tremor. "I simply can't believe my little girl is going to jail."

"They call it the state farm. It sounds better," Dina said with a little smile. "Don't worry about me, Mom. I'll be okay."

"Why did you do it? Why?" Mrs. Stacey turned around and faced her daughter. She had been asking Dina the same question ever since the court trial.

"I've told you. I just had to do it. That's all. I can't explain it anymore."

"Maybe you were right," Mrs. Stacey said, tears in her eyes. "Maybe you were right, and we were wrong. I'm going to miss you. . . ."

"I'll miss you too." Dina gave her mother a hug. She felt sorry for her, and close too, although she knew that from now on they would be more like strangers to each other than ever. "Stan is coming over. I wish he'd hurry."

"He's coming now. Here's his car," Mrs. Stacey said from the window.

Dina ran downstairs to greet him, grateful that her mother was tactful enough to remain upstairs so that they could be alone.

"You look terrific. Just the same as always," Stan said to her admiringly.

"Why should I look different?" Dina asked with a smile.

"No reason. You're a terrific girl."

"Thank you. You had a lot to do with the way things turned out. Remember when I got so mad at you, because you wouldn't fight about your hair. I thought you were a coward. I was wrong. The clothes stuff isn't all that important. It's how you feel inside. I've been wanting to tell you that."

"That's okay. Dina, when you come out, will you come down to school for a weekend? There's a big weekend in February."

Dina's eyes lighted up. "That's nice, Stan. That'll give me something to look forward to."

"Are you scared?"

"Of course, I'm scared. Who wouldn't be? But as long as I'm right and I know what I'm doing, they have no power over me."

"Who do you mean?" Stan asked.

"The people who try to push us around. The people who pick on teen-agers, and smash up their own cars, and get drunk and beat up their wives; the people who preach one thing and do another."

"I know. Harry would be proud of you, Dina."

"Thank you, Stan."

"What are you going to do, when you come out?"

Dina shrugged. "I don't know. I haven't told anyone yet, but I won't be coming back here. I'll find a job and try to get into school next fall. I want to be on my own."

"That'll be great." They looked at each other for several seconds. Then, wordlessly, Stan took her in his arms and kissed her. "I'll be around," he said and kissed her again.

"I'm glad." They both saw the unobtrusive car pull into the driveway, and from the window they watched the policewoman step out. "I guess I've got to go," she said to Stan. "Good-bye." And she gave him a last kiss.

Dina ran upstairs for her small suitcase and kissed her mother good-bye.

She went into the kitchen and said good-bye to Hattie, who was weeping. "Don't cry, Hattie. I'll be all right," Dina said, giving her a hug and a kiss.

Her step was light and firm as she got into the car, although her heart was beating nervously. She had never imagined herself leaving home this way, yet she had no regret for the stand she had taken. The ending had come to a tragic event. Her fears now were of a kind that she could cope with—the natural fears of a sheltered girl going to a state prison farm—but she had an inner strength that enabled her to face the future with confidence.

"I'm ready," she said to the woman beside her, and even managed a wry smile.

HILA COLMAN was born and grew up in New York City, where she went to the Calhoun School. After graduation, she attended Radcliffe College. Before she started writing for herself, she wrote publicity material and ran a book club. About fourteen years ago she sold her first story to the *Saturday Evening Post*, and since then her stories and articles have appeared in many periodicals. Some have been dramatized for television. In recent years she has turned to writing books for teen-age girls. One of them, *The Girl from Puerto Rico*, was given a special citation by the Child Study Association of America.

Mrs. Colman and her husband live in Bridgewater, Connecticut. They have two sons, one of whom is married.